ALSO BY SARAH BRUNI

The Night Gwen Stacy Died

MASS
MOTHERING

MASS
MOTHERING

A Novel

SARAH BRUNI

Henry Holt and Company
New York

Henry Holt and Company
Publishers since 1866
120 Broadway
New York, New York 10271
www.henryholt.com

EU Representative: Macmillan Publishers Ireland Ltd., 1st Floor, The Liffey Trust
Centre, 117–126 Sheriff Street Upper, Dublin 1, DO1 YC43

A version of sections of Part 1 was published as "Imagine Every
Light Is a Woman Who Came to the City Alone" in *Boston Review* as
part of its Global Dystopias project on November 3, 2017.

Library of Congress Cataloging-in-Publication Data

Names: Bruni, Sarah, author.
Title: Mass mothering : a novel / Sarah Bruni.
Description: First edition. | New York : Henry Holt and Company, 2026.
Identifiers: LCCN 2025014139 | ISBN 9781250392619 (hardcover) |
  ISBN 9781250392602 (ebook)
Subjects: LCGFT: Fiction | Novels
Classification: LCC PS3602.R848 M37 2026 | DDC 813/.6—dc23/
  eng/20250602
LC record available at https://lccn.loc.gov/2025014139

Our books may be purchased in bulk for promotional, educational, or business
use. Please contact your local bookseller or the Macmillan Corporate and
Premium Sales Department at (800) 221-7945, extension 5442, or by e-mail at
MacmillanSpecialMarkets@macmillan.com.

First Edition 2026

Printed in the United States of America

1   2   3   4   5   6   7   8   9   10

To Andrés and Ezio

MASS
MOTHERING

I

Note to future readers:

What follows are excerpts from my working translation of
Field Notes, the posthumous book by Tomas Petritus, unfinished
at the time of his death. In his notes, the author referred to
the genre of his writing as "field notes," or elsewhere, simply
as "prose." The story is factual, based on recorded testimonies,
though prior to Petritus's death, fragments of it were serially
published, as often was the case with true crime. The most
complete biography of the author published in any language
is this one: *Tomas Petritus attended the oldest university in the
Baltic States, earning a doctorate in Understudied Languages and
Literatures. He lived abroad for most his life and died of natural
causes at the age of seventy-three.*

I offer these pages with the caveat that I do not consider
myself to be a professional translator. I dedicated myself to this
project as a pure exercise with no interest in seeking publication
for it, although it's true that I did receive some financial
assistance for this work in the form of a federally funded arts
grant at one point. Though I acquired a working knowledge of
the language of Petritus's book years ago, I greatly improved my
technical proficiency in the language through the viewing of
movies that I illegally downloaded from the Internet during a
period of convalescence.

—A.

FIELD NOTES

August 4

The mothers stand in a circle in the central square and fan themselves with the daily news. Sometimes when a cloud passes, they unfold the ridges in their fans and skim a few paragraphs to check if anything true has been printed since yesterday. They are armed with umbrellas to temper the effects of the sun. As seen from the belfry of the cathedral, you'd think it was raining—but it isn't, it doesn't.

An umbrella is a shade. A newspaper is a fan.

A mother is a mother, regardless of the latest information regarding her child.

The mothers wear blue jeans and sleeveless shirts, flip-flop sandals, gold necklaces that spell their names or their children's names or that feature the human forms of saints. They're younger than they look. Not a single one over thirty-six. They have long eyelashes, long hair, short strides, thin waists.

I watch as each of them embraces the others. When they do, their colorful umbrellas shift to create new patterns, fit together like seamless tessellations. By my count from the belfry, there are maybe twenty of them down there. Later I'll review the footage to record an exact figure.

The meeting is consistent with typical protocol as far as I've observed. Each time one of their sons is reported as a missing person at the local precinct, the mothers gather here to embrace, recite prayers, throw rocks, smoke cigarettes, curse under their breath, weep, stare into space.

Typical protocol is they take turns mothering whoever is at her weakest.

August 12

According to my records, the year of the disappearances started calmly, regularly, without any sense of alarm, confusion, illusion, or aberration in the normal sequence of time passing. The 47 bus passed every day at 5 p.m., and Kings and Servants Tavern opened its doors for business at the same hour. When the Sisters of Our Holy Ghost pushed the last Glory Be of beads through their fingers for the night and latched shut the heavy doors of the cathedral, Madame O pulled out her folding table and lawn chair. Shuffling her tarot deck, she read the futures written inside the palms of passersby on the sidewalk by the light of the streetlamp that fell on the patch of concrete between the cathedral and the post office in the central square. The mail—contrary to perceptions in the capital—arrived on schedule, more or less. Packages sometimes took longer or showed up having been rummaged through before crossing the border, but they arrived is the point. The kids were going to school. When they came home, the mothers asked them what they had learned, and the kids rattled off math formulas with orders of operations that made no sense to anyone, which only seemed to serve as evidence that the new generation was learning in ways that were superior to the ways that we had learned, as Lira explained to me during subsequent interviews.

But looking back on it now, it's easy to find signs that things were not right:

Mimi remembered how her hair had stopped growing that spring, how it had begun to knot at the ends, tiny sequences of dead roots giving up, saying enough already. Juliet saw how the stray cat that lived on the block stopped drinking the yogurt she sometimes smuggled from the shelves of the corner store to leave out for it at night. Like a cat that had trusted her all its life decided suddenly that she was trying to poison it. Gloria had started to have dreams in which the principal actors were giant birds of prey that had replaced the heads of state after having acquired the cognitive and motor functions necessary to govern the populace.

Women started seeing the faces of their dead husbands when they closed their eyes. Their husbands were gesticulating wildly, angrily; they were trying to say something that frightened them, but the women could never quite make it out before the images of their husbands were gone.

These are some of the main examples that come to mind. There are others of course.

One might be tempted to note that these observations lean heavily on informants who are women, but I would invite all would-be challengers to visit the town for themselves, install themselves within the central community spaces with clandestine recording devices, and conduct thorough investigations to determine whether they can find much evidence of male inhabitants. Women and children account for the near total population.

People had been disappearing for a long time, but the new pattern, more specifically, goes something like this:

Girls and the occasional grandmother sit around in the central square, play gin rummy, play dominoes, play chess, play canasta.

Boys play dead.

Mothers imagine boys playing dead. Mothers imagine boys dead.

Back and forth like this, ad nauseam. Mothers imagine the bones of boys beginning to calcify in one of the mass graves that everyone knows are waiting to be exhumed on the other side of the mountain range that separates this town from another town from another town that all share the exact same story. And so on across the interior.

August 17

Most days here are the same. I wake up early and start knocking on doors. I pull my recording device from my backpack, and the mothers speak into it, their eyes heavy on the little red light that gives proof of their voices converting into a hard record.

Today, I encountered Lexus on the street with a heavy drawstring sack balanced over her left shoulder. I offered to carry her laundry the remaining two blocks, and over the course of that trajectory, I was able to obtain her written consent to be interviewed. When we arrived at the laundromat at the corner of Hieroglyph and Eighteenth, I set her heavy drawstring sack on one of the folding tables, and I placed my recording device beside it.

It is common knowledge that the disappearances started with her son, Milo. One day he was in the central square playing kickball after school with the sons of the other mothers, and the next day he was gone.

Milo's clothes were in the sack, but she didn't wash them. She said she doesn't want to waste the soap on washing the clothes of someone who has disappeared, because she doesn't want to get up her expectation that he will be coming back. Also, the clothes still have his smell in them.

I watched as Lexus breathed heavily into the cotton T-shirt that had been Milo's, sat back in the plastic deck chair, folded the T-shirt again.

While Lexus waited for the spin cycle to finish with the clothes of every other confirmed living member of her family, she held Milo's clothes up to her face and inhaled the fabric. He was fifteen when he went missing. He is sixteen now, if he is anything other than a lump in the ground.

I listened to Lexus while she described inhaling the fabric of Milo's shirt: musty, musky, alive with a quick smell that keeps mutating and overpowers all her other senses, makes the back of her throat taste of salt.

August 25

This morning, I stopped in a café to sit with a tea and look over my notes. I noticed some whispering as I took my seat, but I mostly tried to ignore it. Over the course of the last few weeks, I have grown used to the stares I draw in public: first, for being an outsider; then, for being a man. I know that the mothers exchange their own notes with one another, so in my interactions with each one of them, I am courteous to a fault. I never raise my voice. I also try to refrain from spitting on the sidewalk, improperly disposing of rubbish, or engaging in any other activity that might identify me as suspect.

When the waitress stood before me with a tray in her hand, she set a cup and saucer down in front of me. Then, she placed a small glass of still water beside it. I thanked her, but I noticed her linger.

She waited for my gaze to lift to her eyes, then she said quietly, almost a whisper, May I sit?

I closed my notebook and stood to push back the chair opposite me, creating a space for her at the table.

She sat down and said, You should talk to Sofia.

As the waitress—*Arlene* is scrawled on the name tag pinned to her breast—explained it, Sofia's son Daniel was the sixth or seventh boy to go missing. He walked to the corner store for a soda and never came home. Since then, Sofia wakes each night to find dead boys in her house, but none of them are Daniel. Arlene and the other mothers take turns keeping watch with her to ward off unfamiliar ghosts.

She's being haunted, Arlene said. I was there the last time it happened.

Do you mind speaking on record? I asked.

Arlene assented, and told me the following story:

There were three of us there that night sprawled around her living room, looking out for her. Sofia woke up claiming to find a dead boy slumped in the corner of the bathtub. She said the boy's neck was broken. That a school of minnows swam around the curves in his hipbones and heels. That she put her hand into the water to touch his wrist and watched the minnows dodge her fingers.

We all peered into the doorway of the bathroom.

Sofia looked from us to the tub again, and it seemed for a moment that she saw what we saw there: nothing.

He was here, she said. In the water.

So we showed her how there was also no water. The shallow tub was dry, and its dull porcelain gleamed. No water, no minnows, no boy.

It's going to be like this for a while, we reminded her. The doctors warned us we might see things.

We approached the tub, tried to embrace her, but Sofia went outside to smoke.

When she came back into the house, we had mostly fallen asleep on the sofa with our shoes still on our feet. Sofia locked the back door and walked into the bathroom. She wiped her eyes and washed her face. When her face was sunken into the bowl of the sink, she said that was when the splashing sounds started up again, just like before.

Sofia approached the tub and pushed her fingers through his long hair. It was when her fingers caught a snag in his hair that she saw how his hair was very fine and light, completely unlike her son's, which was dark and wavy and took hours with a brush to work through its most uncooperative parts. She took off her clothes and climbed into the shallow tub. Displaced, the water sloshed over the edges onto the floor for a second, and then: nothing. She fell asleep like that, her chin in the crook of the boy's neck.

She said that she slept in the tub all night pushing her fingers through his hair—the pretty, docile, nothing hair that wasn't her son's. When she woke up to us knocking on the door hours later, there was no water, no boy. Naked in an empty tub, she stood up and made her way toward the door. We opened our arms to receive her, wrapped her in a beach towel, and led her to the living room, where we kept watch with her for the rest of the night.

When we take care of Sofia, we keep the TV on in the background, just in case we get drowsy, just in case we run out of things to say. The TV offers a different kind of comfort because it is always on, a constant, even on the nights when we cannot be with her.

Sofia's voice grows loud late at night. It's not always clear whether she's talking to us or the TV when she cries out.

To this, we always say, Hush, knead the skin around her shoulders into our palms like dough, and wrap the beach towel tighter around her bare arms.

With that, Arlene paused. She looked at the watch on her wrist and started to stand, clearing away my empty cup. I stood beside her, asked her if she had more to say, her own story to tell.

Of course, she said. But my break is over.

Before standing up and smoothing her hands over her apron, she pressed a small scrap of paper with Sofia's phone number into my hand.

When I was a girl, Sofia explained to me later that same day, during our first recorded interview, my father worked the night shift driving a taxi. It was his second job, he was backup for the regular drivers. They only called him when they needed an extra man on the road. In the morning at breakfast, I would ask my mother if my father had left the house to drive the taxi during the night. If she said yes, I would always confirm that I had already registered this fact somewhere inside my senses; I would always remember the house feeling a little emptier while I slept. That's what it feels like, waking up without the ghost of someone else's boy, even though he is not mine and only shares very basic physical characteristics with my boy.

End of tape.

From this moment on, I recognize that my relationship to Sofia's life will be fleeting but persistent. I know that to her I am only the man who shows up, takes notes, draws conclusions, flies back to the capital. For this reason, I'm doing the best I can to stay out of the way of Lexus's and Sofia's grief while still picking up on the most salient details that fit with the patterns I have observed to date. I try to record everything I can as faithfully as possible. I

SARAH BRUNI

know I cannot fathom the kind of grief that they have known, so I don't pretend to try. I have weathered my own losses of course, but mostly through the fault of my own pride and inattention to the things that matter. If I am being honest with myself, the truth is that I sometimes wish that I hadn't started talking to the mothers, that I could go back to being someone who is unencumbered by their stories. But once I decided to be an open receptor to them, more mothers kept coming forward to speak. Though I know I am a coward compared to the courage that exists in any one of their pinkie fingernails, I have already begun the process of documentation.

September 1

Life in the capital doesn't preoccupy itself with the problems of the small provincial towns like that of my research site. It's inadvisable to speak plainly of multinational militarized apparatuses that can be positively correlated to some trends we might want to discuss at some point, so no one is going to say anything even remotely close to that. It's as easy as shifting focus.

For example:

In the capital, there are minor earthquakes that happen every day. No big deal. The only reason you can feel them at all in the capital is because of the height of the living towers. The buildings sway for a moment, just long enough to make you wonder, and then they groan and settle back in place. Usually nothing happens. The official messaging is: Go out onto your private balcony. Take some deep breaths. Admire the formations of the distant mountains. In other words, it's better not to think about the fact that entire living towers have collapsed this way—building permits don't always take into account plate tectonics. It can be a logistical nightmare to comply with all the standards, all the red tape.

At night, views from private balconies are phenomenal. The mountains glimmer in the distance as thousands of stray lights switch on after sunset. You might convert the dazzling image into a practical understanding of its composite like this: Imagine every light is a woman. Imagine every light is a woman who came to the capital alone. That's pretty much an exact mathematical ratio of what's going on here. Behind each faraway light is an internal alien settlement. Eighty percent of breadwinners in internal alien households are single mothers—disenfranchised young women uprooted from the interior of the country, who, nevertheless, possess clear knowledge of how to illegally rig electrical currents to reach neighborhoods that the municipal authorities do not service. We've all seen the billboards featuring the blurred face of a woman with a live wire in each hand. The slogan *Think internal aliens aren't stealing your electricity? Think again!* has become ubiquitous.

Around the same time that malls started going up, all the colonial architecture was ripped from its foundations in favor of the living towers, which have come to be the preferred residential arrangements in a place where one is careful about who one meets. The gym and pool and children's birthday party space are all contained within the central courtyard. Building management emphasizes that it is all constructed with extreme convenience in mind. For instance:

Here are the areas where it's permitted to hang up balloons and streamers.

Here is the hookup for the stereo and karaoke machine.

If you choose to sing songs with profane lyrics, your neighbors are liable to complain to management and hold you accountable. In the tower where I've been staying for the past few weeks while I compile notes, for instance, the management considers the development of a respectful community to be paramount.

Make sure that you request to reserve the central courtyard for your private event at least two weeks prior to the date. Other rules include:

Pick up after your pets.

Swim at your own risk.

No running, no diving, no horseplay.

No shirt, no shoes, no service.

Now that you have all these rules to keep in mind, can you even remember the names of any towns in the interior? Could you locate them on a map? As for the names of the temporary settlements in the surrounding mountains, it's more common to refer to these areas by their capital-assigned numbers. On the nightly news, citizens are cautioned to avoid settlements 12, 25, and 36, for example, at all costs.

September 9

The town of the mothers is different from the places where they were born and where their parents were buried, places whose names have lain dormant, curled up in the roofs of their mouths like secrets for so long they're almost gone. These places still exist on the map, but it would be better to pretend otherwise. Besides, maps lie. The black dots that locate the site and relative density of towns, for example, appear identical before and after massacres. The mothers have started to remove the names of their towns from their vocabularies.

Instead, they remember them through tastes and, sometimes, old smells on the air that disorient and confuse: salt mixed with dirt, fried meat with pollen.

Last week Mimi walked to town from halfway up a mountain with a fistful of wildflowers and a crazed look in her eyes.

Come here, hurry up! she yelled to the mothers, pushing the flowers into their faces.

They inhaled, but noticed nothing, nothing outside the realm of every other wildflower they've smelled in their lives.

It's gone, Mimi agreed. It's all used up. But when I was walking, I passed some horses—

She broke off, smiled, nestled the half-dead bouquet in her arms like a bride.

But she didn't have to say anything else. Even if their old homes have nothing to do with wildflowers, with horses. It's an easy correlation, all the mothers agree.

The days when they pause to breathe so deeply that all the smells around them mix, they feel most lost. That hint of a whiff of the familiar stings their nostrils, makes home feel close and nowhere at once.

September 14

Their stories often start like this:

Someone gave my husband a bag of seeds.

Miriam was the one speaking to me, but the other mothers nodded. The ruin of a family starts slowly. Only later do the mothers trace it back to the crops that quietly spelled trouble beneath the soil.

He took the seeds because our land was destroyed, Miriam continued. We spent years trying with tubers and barleys and lettuces. Nothing grew. I had five children who lived on broth and sometimes rice and almost no meat. My husband came home one day after several meetings with a stern look on his face. He asked me, How would you like to see this place covered in green leaves? At first, there was nothing I wanted more. But these leaves, you can't feed them to your children. I saw he had already made up his mind, though. I conjured up a field of green leaves and small white flowers, like those I'd seen already growing nearby in the small plots of neighbors. Then my husband leaned in close and whispered to me the selling prices as they were told to him, and I whispered these numbers back to him to be sure I had heard him right. My husband pushed the bag into my hands. I was the one who planted the first seeds. I planted them with resolve and imagined staying put. I buried them and I thought of my mother, of how when we put her in the ground I expected my family would stay on the land where she was. My family has been running for half a century or more. A history of running is what I share with all my traceable ancestors. This is why when the seeds came to my husband they seemed the answer to a prayer.

Miriam's face slowed and fell. She pushed her forehead into the shoulder of another mother, Eli, who turned to me and summarized the end of the memory in a few words as if by rote, because it is also her story:

Yeah, she said. Some prayer.

Eli stopped, shook her head, but there is no record of this gesture.

End of tape.

I used to be a believer is a sentence I have documented many times in my research.

Faith dissolves at different moments for different informants. One popular example is the moment when the youngest children, the ones just learning how to run, start dropping dead in the fields.

Look up. Overhead, low-flying planes dust crops with a foreign toxin specially formulated to decimate the growth of these green leaves.

Aside from leading to the demise of plants, flowers, animals, and small children, the substance has also been correlated with uncorroborated reports of symptoms including: rashes, headaches, dizziness, fainting spells, dry eyes, dry mouth, shortness of breath, blood clots, irritable bowel syndrome, infections of the liver, infections of the bloodstream, kidney failure, heart failure, strokes, boils on the skin, blurred vision.

Still, official literature published on the topic advises the citizenry to acknowledge that uncorroborated correlations are not the same as facts.

September 23

In the home of Sandra, the mothers gather weekly to voice different hypothetical scenarios. Some get listed aloud, and some get
listed without words inside the quiet of their bodies. Scenarios
include: Their boys found steady jobs in the next province and
have been working so hard that they haven't had the chance to
write home. Or, their boys all fell in love and eloped. Or, their
boys have gone to look for their fathers. Or, their boys are being
held hostage somewhere.

The possibility that the boys lie quiet in one of the stretches of
land where the mothers observe haggard scavenger birds making
excruciatingly slow circles in the sky is one example of a scenario
that is not voiced aloud.

Juliet's boy said to her before he left: I found a job in the capital.
I'll be gone for a few months, but not forever. I'll send home as
much help as I can.

But that was nine months ago. He's never called or written,
never sent a dime. Juliet checks the mail every day to be sure.

* * *

When Joel went missing, the mothers squeezed Gloria's hands in theirs. Then, they locked themselves into their bedrooms to cry until they could not breathe.

They do not talk about the fact that is clear to everyone, that Joel did not leave town to find work. The complications when he was born have caused him to learn to speak later than the other boys, so that even at seventeen he speaks slowly, loudly. He cannot perform simple math functions. He does not understand the value of money.

Instead, hypothetical scenarios #57, #58, and #59 are added to the running list:

The boys are lost in the mountains. The boys fell ill while traveling and are being hospitalized in small towns not unlike this one. The boys crossed paths with a rebel camp in the woods, where they are being temporarily held purely for administrative purposes.

September 30

For the benefit of my comprehension, the mothers elaborate on the relationships among themselves:

We call each other sweetie, baby, mama, skinny, love, little thing, my dear, honey, artichoke, plum.

We make each other sweet tea, flavored water, coffee, juice, lemonade.

We go to the corner to fetch one another's cigarettes, sodas, liquors, chocolates.

We fold each other's sheets, prepare each other's dinners, discipline each other's daughters, sing each other's lullabies.

Our care for each other is intuitive, obvious as breast milk.

End of tape.

October 3

I dreamed of Queenie again last night. In the dream she is floating on her back in the sea, and I am watching her from the shore. Every time a wave crests over her body, I verify that her head surfaces again. Just before I wake up, I'm ankle-deep in the water shouting her name. But Queenie is from the coast, a village where the river and sea meet—she swims expertly, easily. She hasn't seen an ocean in years. When she migrated to the mountains, she couldn't sleep at first because of all the missing sounds. Or, at least, that's what I've been told by the other mothers. She is one mother I cannot push far from my brain, even on gray mornings in the capital, when I am heating coffee on the stove and have not yet pulled out my notes to transcribe the latest rounds of interviews.

Before Queenie appeared in my notes, it was her daughter Zara who approached me. It was during the raw afternoon hours when the air is too thick to move through. I had picked up a soda at the corner store that faces the facade of the cathedral, and I was sitting on a nearby bench to drink it, when Zara sat on the bench beside me. A girl of maybe eight or nine in a blue jumper and white shirt—the local school uniform.

There were other girls in the same school jumpers in the square, sitting in a circle with a fat piece of chalk in their fingers that they kept passing around and adding to something written in the middle of their circle that I couldn't see.

Zara sat next to me the way you might sit beside a statue or a tree stump without acknowledging its presence. Her legs were too short to fold over the end of the bench toward the ground. Instead, the heels of her shoes indicated straight ahead, toward the circle of girls. She studied them blankly, without fear of being observed back.

Why aren't you with them? I asked.

Zara looked at me for a second, squinted her eyes a little in the corners, then turned her attention back to the circle of girls.

I didn't think she was going to respond at all, but a few minutes later she turned to me and laughed, very quietly, under her breath.

You talk wrong, she said.

I come from very far away, I said.

Zara shrugged. Then why don't you go home?

We met again a few days later, around the same hour in the square, on the bench that faces the cathedral. Zara sat down beside me again, though there were other empty benches in the square.

I'm going to the corner to buy some sodas, I said. Are you thirsty?

Zara stared ahead at the girls inside the circle of chalk.

Grape soda?

Nothing.

Lemon?

She frowned.

Orange?

She nodded, almost imperceptibly.

One orange soda coming right up, I said.

But when I came back to the bench, she was gone.

As I drank her soda, I walked from the shadow of the bench to the blaring sun of the center of the square. I walked in a straight line as if about to enter the nave of the cathedral, but on my way, I passed by the circle of girls. Inside their circle of crossed legs, I read the words:

Traitors (in reverse-alphabetical order) = Theo, Max, Adrian, Anderson, _____.

The girls passed the chalk and smiled to one another. I heard giggling as I walked by and stopped in front of the facade, which I pretended to stupidly admire, in order to keep them within earshot.

They said nothing.

October 6

They miss their mothers.

Their mothers would know what to do. But the mothers' mothers were buried in the towns they fled. Or their mothers didn't support their decisions to have the babies of the men who had become their husbands, and they had just lost touch. Or they suspected their mothers were dead but because they had never seen the bodies with their own eyes, they didn't discuss this, not even with their own children. Or their mothers had been gathered up with all their fathers in fields as they sat blindfolded on the steps of a nearby cathedral, and the last thing they remember was pushing the flats of their palms into their ears. Or, in very rare cases, they still share a bed with their mothers at night.

Their mothers smelled the same as always the last time they embraced them: like bar soap, day-old bread, lavender, kitchen grease. Their eyes sting on days when they turn a corner too fast and are met with the yeast or soap smells that remind them of their mothers.

Miriam remembers how her mom used to drag the sign of the cross into her forehead whenever she left the house. She must have used the corner of her fingernail because sometimes it had left a mark in her powdered face. If Miriam complained, her mother had pressed her nail in harder.

Lira's mom had patched up the holes in her clothes. She'd never asked her mother to do this. She would put on the same pair of jeans in the morning that she took off the night before, and notice the wind didn't pass through the knees anymore.

Queenie's had sung in the shower. She'd had a gravelly deep voice like the bottom of a river. When Queenie tries to sing her mom's songs, the words sound too thin in her mouth.

Juliet still shares a bed with her mom at night. Her mother talks in her sleep, old stories that come out mixed with snores so loud that Juliet barely sleeps. Juliet has become beautiful with an enviable set of permanent dark circles around her eyes at all times that grow with each night she lies awake listening to her mother.

Mimi explained, When we greet Juliet in line at the grocery, we look away at piled fruits and hanging meats to avoid her eyes.

They miss their husbands.

They miss how their husbands grabbed their waists and pulled them closer to them in their beds at night. Their husbands, with their dirty fingernails and flat feet, with their distrust of saints and superstitions, with their chests and arms.

The way they yelled at the radio.

The way they tore apart the house looking for something that was in the same place as always.

The way they changed their voices when they talked to animals.

Their husbands left them with children, with bruises on their bodies, with the smells of their shaving lotions in the bathroom, with rings on their fingers or in their ears.

Sometimes the mothers used to say they wished their husbands would leave for good, but now that they are gone, it is different:

Their husbands left them for younger women, or they were kidnapped, or they stepped on explosives, or they starved to death in the hills, or they were gunned down at home while everyone slept, or they were in the capital trying to save enough to send for them, or they were already so long in the ground it was pointless to try to remember the sounds of their voices.

Sometimes they think about the days when their husbands were still strangers. When a girlfriend had said how she'd seen him staring this way, how they'd rolled their eyes and laughed. How they thought at first, No way: too short. Or, Too skinny. Or, Talks too much, my god, thinks he knows everything. How the first time their husbands spoke to them—in the park, or in the church, or in the field—and the words came out rushed because of a trembling mouth.

Sometimes they imagine what might have happened if they hadn't smiled, or turned around, or listened to the rest of what the men who would become their husbands had wanted to say to them.

They miss their boys.

At night is the worst. From inside their beds and bodies, they speak to the ceiling with voices that rise and fall at the pitch of wounded animals left for dead in the fields. Starvation is what eventually quiets the animals.

The mothers stay ravenous.

October 7

The next day, Zara was already on the bench when I approached her with an orange soda.

I twisted off the cap and passed it to her. She gulped at it like someone wandering the desert, half-dazed by passing mirages.

Thirsty? I asked.

Yes, sir, she said in her bird's voice.

Why don't you sit with the other girls? I asked.

Zara went silent again.

After a few minutes passed she said, I know who you are.

Oh, I said. Who?

You talk to the moms, she said. You're the old man that talks to the moms.

I'm forty-two, I said. That's not so old.

It is here, she said.

I came to tell you to stay away from her.

That's the first thing that Queenie ever said to me. I didn't have my recording device with me that day, so I'm writing this conversation to the best of my memory.

Every time a strange man shows up here, it spells trouble, Queenie said.

I come with only a notebook, I said.

The last one came with seeds, she said.

Queenie walked away, left me standing alone in the dust and heat of the square.

A.

I have always been intimidated by mothers. They fascinate and repel me because they know a kind of fierce, animal love that I do not. On the train, I could always feel their knowing, judging eyes on me: when I wore impractical shoes, when I was resting a heavy, important novel on my lap, when I fell asleep instead of being vigilant in the task of seeing if there were any of them in the vicinity who needed my seat.

This summer I pretend to be one of them. I become the care-taker for a four-year-old boy. I thought I would earn some sort of surrogate respect from their kind, but mothers are smart. They can sniff out impostors. I have the fresh face of a babysitter in spite of my thirty-three years.

The boy I care for is named R. He likes to watch the trains go by on the opposite track. He likes to sit in his own seat, even at rush hour. He likes to stand up from his seat at odd moments and hug the legs of strangers. I let R. do what he wants to because every day we ride the train straight from his school, where I pick him up, to his classes in speech therapy and the acquisi-tion of motor skills. He is a boy who has to work hard for all the things many people do not—walk without braces, feed himself, communicate verbally. When he hugs the legs of commuters, some of them (men, women with impractical shoes) give me a look of *control your kid*. When the commuters whose legs he hugs belong to mothers, it is immediately apparent, because they come down to his level and give him full hugs, or they say, Thanks honey, I needed that. They don't even bother with me. They communicate directly with R.

These are the kinds of actions that distinguish mothers from the rest of the population.

If R. finishes with his therapy early and it is one of the long summer afternoons, we go on excursions together. We ride the train to the history museum. We make slow laps around a room with a blue whale suspended from the ceiling. (R. dodges and I chase and intercept him before he hugs the legs of unsuspecting tourists.) We lie flat on our backs side by side and stare into the belly of the whale like it is a faraway constellation that could be deciphered for counsel regarding our lives on land. It is exhilarating and exhausting, although I experience only a fraction of the exhilaration and exhaustion that R.'s mother knows. I see it in the way her eyes become soft when R. walks into the room, the way R. makes the sign for *mom* over and over again with his hands whenever she comes home.

At night, I read to R. to help him fall asleep. We like to read books about wild animals who wind up in metropolitan settings. There is a crocodile that lives with a family in a neighborhood of pristine brownstones and helps the stay-at-home mother with her daily chores. There is a bear that wanders around a department store in the middle of the night. Our favorite book is about a lion that is lost in the suburbs and asks all the townspeople for directions back to his home in the local zoo. No one listens to the lion. They scream and run away and try to bring in the National Guard to shoot tranquilizer darts into its fur. A boy, the only human being in town who is not afraid, finally intervenes and offers to walk the lion home.

When I ask R. if he liked the books we read, he nods, or he makes the sign for *more*, or he walks from his bed and retrieves another book from his shelf. When R. falls asleep, I kiss his forehead and tiptoe into the living room, where I pass out reading my own books, waiting for his mother to get home.

When she arrives, R.'s mother shakes me awake, and I walk out of the building in a daze, smile a sleepy *good night* to the doorman, and ride the train home. At that hour, commuters have aprons and uniforms balled up in their hands. The fluorescent lights and overhead ads accost us, exhaust us; we lean into one another's bodies with every shift and curve. Our ears pop in the tunnels underwater. Some of us fall asleep and miss our stops. The ads overhead evaluate whether we deserve to be here, whether we belong here, whether we are transients, whether this city is ours.

The ads ask questions like, *Is your dog a* real *city resident?*

If the answer is yes, it will be necessary to register our pets with the city, get them some rabies shots, finance the removal of their reproductive organs.

Made in the city! is written across a cropped photo of a woman's cleavage. The prices for different payment plans dart across the area where we imagine the dark of her nipples.

Some organs must be removed; some organs must be enhanced. The ads suggest to us that if we deserve to live here, we'd instinctively know the difference. We'd have a local's intuition.

I don't have a local's intuition. I have the kind of history that is easy to erase and not notice anything is gone. When my great-grandparents emigrated from four different countries, their shared goal was rapid assimilation. As a result, I am third-generation nothing. If someone asks me, Where are you from, I mean, originally? I say, Nowhere, USA. When I travel back to the miles of cornfields and strip malls where I was raised, I easily get lost.

The summer I find Petritus's book is the same summer that young men and boys are killed every few weeks in every major city, and we all watch it happen through live-streamed videos on our handheld devices. I offer this as a kind of explanation: By the time I find the mothers' stories, I am already half-sick from watching the faces of mothers here on the news each night.

It's a hot summer. Air conditioners drip water onto our heads from windows overhead. Box fans hum. Public pools are at capacity. Drug stores sell out of ice. Men of all ages lick their lips and catcall anything walking.

To me, they say things like, You look like a good snack. Or, Take me with you wherever you're going tonight, beautiful.

Sometimes I smile at them and sometimes I scowl at some hazy point of focus I train my eyes on in the distance. Sometimes I yell back. If it's late at night, I am ashamed to admit I have half-crossed my eyes, let my tongue hang from the side of my mouth, and walked in a zigzag while muttering a steady stream of audible expletives under my breath.

When I mention to my mother that I do this to dispel male attention, she is horrified.

What a way to live! she says.

This is one of her favorite expressions. The implication is that it would be more reasonable to conduct my life in a place not unlike the one where I was raised, where everyone travels in vehicles and not on foot, in the heat, or visible to the naked eyes of onlookers.

I had been living in the city for almost a decade when I went in for routine tests at my doctor's office and my life started to resemble someone else's. It started as a scare that showed up out of nowhere, introduced six months of strained conversations with a revolving entourage of medical professionals about expelling the malignant growth the scare had revealed, and left me with a long scar along the underside of my abdomen. It was fortunate that this potentially life-threatening abnormality showed up early, unexpectedly, in routine lab work. A fortunate find, repeated all the medical professionals, very fortunate. But, even so, by the time the scare transformed itself into a scar, I had lost every adjunct section of Language Elective for Non-Native Speakers I taught at the community center, the contents of my bank account, the sum of my reproductive organs, my interest in romantic relationships, my will to perform routine tasks such as getting out of bed, going grocery shopping, or answering the phone. I had always imagined that I would have plenty of time to make my own decisions over questions of mothering: namely, whether I would become a mother, when, and how. The abnormal cells showed up inside me and were removed so quickly I didn't have time to adjust and reconsider before the surgery was complete and my future determined, blank and open: unencumbered as an empty agenda.

After long weeks spent flat on my back alone in a studio apartment, I'd found the job with R. to pay my rent and fill my hours again during the day. At night, I went dancing alone. When I got tired, I took the train home alone. I was surprised to find that my legs could still carry me anywhere, easily. I was still a fast walker, long strides. When I went out dancing, I used to look across the bar at anyone I wanted to and dare whoever made eye contact with me to ask me to dance. I was big on dance as communication then. I had some theories about it that I had either read or invented, and at the time, they all seemed 100 percent relevant and true. They gave me license to ignore the long, supportive messages friends left on my voicemail all that winter. They gave me license to stay up late embracing strangers four or five nights a week without guilt about spending money I didn't have. I'd recently paid off educational loans only to fill my credit cards with charges incurred in city hospitals, laboratories, and doctors' offices. As it turned out, each one of these institutions billed separately. The regular practice of reviewing the line-by-line itemization of charges for services with obscure names—like *biopsy of cervical curettage*, and *rapid excision diagnostic procedure*—made the relative number of cover fees I paid to enter bars with music each week seem irrelevant.

Staying up late and entering bars alone at night is how I met N.

N. has small, delicate hands, the size of a woman's, and hair that he keeps tied in a knot at the base of his skull. He laughs with his entire body. Sometimes when the bars close, we walk the city together at night. I link my arm into his, or he links his arm into mine, and we pretend to be tourists and ignore the fact that we both have to be awake in several hours for work. N. likes to practice speaking my language, and I prefer to speak in N.'s language, so we aren't too picky. We reach between the two to find the best and most appropriate words and never have to say, How do you say . . . ? I learned N.'s language at a university in the middle of a cornfield and perfected it talking to my neighbors in peripheral city neighborhoods. But my capacity to understand linguistic nuances was greatly improved by downloading movies in the months following my surgery, flat on my back in bed, my laptop balanced on my thighs. N. learned my language in a trial-by-fire kind of methodology: working as a bicycle delivery boy at nineteen, the age that he got on an airplane with a tourist visa and never went home.

Now N. works at the airport, unloading luggage from the bellies of planes and onto conveyor belts. He goes to the airport every day, but he hasn't been on a plane since the one he boarded eighteen years ago to come here. He is a painter. He stopped painting around the time I stopped returning the messages that accumulated on my voicemail, which gives us both a lot of extra time to run into each other at the same bars on different nights of the week where there is a reliable rotation of cheap live music.

We never communicate our plans ahead of time, we just know: Monday at Telex, Wednesday at Mina's, every other Thursday in the basement bar of Ciel, and Friday at the pier. I always go alone, but I know I will almost always run into N. eventually. I start dancing, and the night reaches the point at which I could be in any city, in any country, in any time zone, in any body, at any time of night. It is always around then, when I am halfway into a stride toward the bar or a dance, when I feel someone grasp my hand. I turn and N. smiles.

Skinny, where are you going?

And I forget where I was going, and he takes my hand that is still grasped in his and guides it to his shoulder, an invitation to dance to whatever song has already started to play.

I told N. my name when we first met, but I never heard him use it. N. gave me his name, but later that night when he was paying for drinks, I heard the bartender call him by a different name.

Whenever the bar closes and the music stops, whichever of us has made a little extra money that week invites the other one to eat french fries and drink chamomile tea in a diner in the middle of the night. We order the chamomile tea because each of our mothers—mine living, his dead—has convinced us that it is the cure for everything. While we nurse the chamomile, we tell each other stories from our other lives, the lives we each lived before this one. When neither of us has money, we sit in parks until we get kicked out by the cops, or until one of us falls asleep on the other's shoulder. Neither of us really ever wants to go home. There are ghosts in both of our houses.

When I was a girl, ghosts and guardian angels occupied principal places in many of the stories my family told me. For example, my mother used to say that both guardian angels and ghosts would do whatever they need to do to get your attention. Let's say you're in a burning building in the middle of the night. Your guardian angel could knock all the picture frames off the walls of your room to wake you up. Or throw stuffed animals at you. Or rip up your books. They don't have any respect for personal property.

Would you rather be burned to a crisp with all your books? my mother used to ask me.

Ghosts function along similar lines, but with different motives. To scare, I supposed. For this reason, and others, as a child I was equally afraid of ghosts and guardian angels.

The ghosts that are in my house now are different. They don't throw things at me; they are silent. They are mostly found in the eyes of the matriarchs of my family. They watch me from the photos I have taped to the walls of my studio apartment. Their looks silently list their sacrifices in light of my life of waste and plenty.

Any guardian angels assigned to me have yet to destroy my books.

Here's one of my family stories that I never tell N.:

Leonora changed her name to Nora as a child when her family immigrated here. I try to insist to the progeny of her siblings that my grandmother's name is Nora, and everyone brushes me away with their hands as if to say, *Quiet down, peon. That story is not relevant.* In the hand-drawn family tree (the one that I had understood up until this point to be a collaborative effort), they write in heavy black ink over my pencil lettering, *Leonora*, so that the name that I call my grandmother is just a graphite shadow under this other name from her past life.

I tell my grandmother this, and she says, Oh well, you know. As if it's something that is none of her business.

But what does it say on your birth certificate? I ask her.

I mean, says my grandmother, we didn't used to pay so much attention to paperwork then. We were just trying to figure out how to survive.

Surviving is something my grandmother had an aptitude for. Before the war, she picked onions in a field for five cents a day. With her earnings that summer, she purchased a long white skirt and an emerald sweater to wear to her first day of school. Later, with her high school degree, she found a steady job in a bank. For fifty years, she wore high heels and pantyhose and shook men's hands. Because she was away all day, my mother was raised mostly by her own grandmother, my great-grandmother, Gaia. Gaia was from a town that hugged the sea; amid the cornfields and strip malls, she learned the new language that was required of her here in a singsong way, gendering all the nouns and adding vowels to the ends of everything.

My grandmother sometimes adds vowels to the ends of things, but she does it with affection, not confusion or necessity. At ninety-three years old, she lives alone; she drives a car; she balances her checkbook to the penny.

Here's one of N.'s family stories he never finished telling me:

N. was the one to find his mom.

Well, I can't exactly tell you this story, because I only know it in parts, the parts that he mentioned here and there. Some of this is conjecture, but this is what I know.

Heart attack. Naked from the waist down. She was wearing a blue blouse, halfway unbuttoned, with large details of butterflies printed on it, and a white lace bra underneath. N. was just a boy when he found her like that in the shower. Her right leg twitched with the smallest repetitive motion that made him think she was going to wake up. How if he could find help in time, she was going to wake up. He and his mother were alone in the house, so he ran to the neighbor's barefoot, the dogs trailing behind him barking.

She didn't die that day, whether thanks to N.'s intervention or her own body's intuition, I can't be sure. I can't remember if I made up the part about the butterflies and the lace and the right leg's repetitive motion, or if this is part of the story as he told it to me. It seems disrespectful to N.'s mother to make up any further details just to tell you the story in a way that would make you feel something of what N. felt, so I'll stop trying.

Instead, I'll keep telling my own stories of immigrants who felt uncomfortable and hungry, who changed some of the official language of legal documents to ease certain transitions, but who always survived, always passed along improved living conditions to whoever was born next.

I was in the grocery store when I got the call from my doctor, who had assured me the week before when I went to him for a routine exam that he'd only call in the case that something irregular came up.

The receptionist asked to speak to me.

Speaking, I said.

Great, I'll put the doctor through.

I guess you're probably wondering why I'm calling, the doctor said.

I paused in front of the rows of cereals. The frantic appeals of their cursive scripts lurched into my vision, offering a balanced start to the day.

The thing is, the doctor said, there seems to be a bit of an irregularity in terms of cell growth. Both adenocarcinoma in situ and squamous cell carcinoma. Could be cancerous or precancerous, but we really don't want to get ahead of ourselves. We won't know much more until we take a sample.

Adeno—, I said.

—carcinoma, said the doctor. Highly irregular for it to show up like this, so it was a pretty lucky find. Could be cause for a radical intervention, could be nothing.

Radical? I repeated.

Oh. Right, the doctor said. Radical just means immediate and diagnostic.

I understand, I said. I cupped my hand over the mouthpiece as if this action might make the call more private. I spoke softly, tenderly, into the top flaps of the cereal boxes, as I scheduled a biopsy, then hung up the phone.

I paced the full length of the aisle and called my mother. It might only be precancerous, I explained brightly, fooling neither of us.

When's the biopsy? my mother asked immediately.

But I already couldn't remember.

I had to call back the doctor's office to ask.

Because I always refuse to let N. come home with me—my apartment feels antiseptic, quiet; it resembles a site of quarantine—N. finally takes me home with him. He lives with an older couple who emigrated from his country twenty years ago, who rented out the bedroom of their one-bedroom apartment to him. They moved their bed out to the living room, and N. sleeps on a pullout sofa in the bedroom. When we go to his apartment, he doesn't turn on a single light. He knows his way through the darkness, past their bed—where I hear the man snoring and sometimes the woman mutters things under her breath in her sleep. They sleep in an embrace, though I try not to notice that or any other intimacy, because I am a stranger in their home in the middle of the night. N. takes my hand and guides me toward his bedroom, silently.

N. and I share a bed several nights a week for eight months, but we don't sleep together, because my body is incapable of being hospitable to another body. It's not something I ever try to explain. It is a fact obvious to N. every time he touches me, and my body goes cold and my mind wanders off somewhere else. Instead, we lie side by side in his bed and we listen to each other's stories, or the parts of each other's stories we are each willing to tell, or that we think the other would like to hear.

I listen as N. tells me about the time that his mother left him alone with his grandparents for a long time, and his grandfather disappeared for four days, until he reappeared, and when N.'s grandmother confronted him about his absence, his grandfather took a pistol out of the waistband of his jeans and shot three bullets through the roof of the family's home. N.'s grandmother took the family to live somewhere else for a month, but N.'s grandfather begged them to return, and when they finally did, N. was the first person to enter the family home again. N.'s grandfather turned to him before anyone else entered the room and said, to him alone—a pact between the men of the house—that the thing that happened in this living room would never happen again, and though his grandfather did not repeat what he said aloud to N.'s grandmother, it was true. N.'s mother returned and the entire family lived peacefully together under this roof with the three patched bullet holes in it until six years later when N.'s grandfather was killed by a drunk driver while walking home from mass.

I listen as N. tells me about the time that he ran into his childhood friend on the street in the middle of the night, someone he had not seen for many years. And his friend's hands were visibly shaking as he said, Come on, let's get a drink, I want to talk to you. And N. felt compelled to go with his friend even though everyone knew this friend had become someone whose hand was always a half gesture away from a gun at his hip. As soon as they were seated at the bar, N.'s friend confessed to him that he'd just been offered a sum of money to hunt down an old schoolmate of theirs. N. shook his head as if to say, Don't do it. But it was already done, that's why he'd come directly to talk to N. He'd already put four bullets in the guy's stomach and watched him bleed to death on the sidewalk, and now he needed help deciding what to do next. So N. sat with him in a bar all night and they slowly drank beers and talked about when they were kids: the half-blind teacher who had mixed up everyone's names; the motherless baby bird they'd tried to teach to fly before someone's brother stepped on it; the unsteady light of the neighborhood playing fields at night. N. was never afraid because he was too busy thinking about the fact that this would be the last time he saw his friend. And N. was right. Two weeks later his friend was gunned down at 2 p.m. walking down the street in front of his mother's house.

At some point I realize that a gun appears in every one of N.'s stories. By the time I meet N., I have spent a lot of time processing stories in his language and in mine—I practically consider myself a professional listener—so I understand that when a gun appears in a story it's only a matter of time before it goes off. This is one of the rules I've learned. There are others.

Sometimes N. tells stories without pauses between them. His stories blur together. He finishes one and starts another without transition. He tells them fast, almost by rote, which makes me wonder sometimes if the stories are really his. If I don't stop him eventually to tell him that I need to sleep so I can go to work in the morning, N. would keep telling me stories all night.

My stories are different. They are mostly about mothers and poets, their bodies and collected works. Mothers and poets are often considered minor. Mothers and poets rarely carry guns. This is one of the reasons that their stories don't capture the imaginations of the consumer public. These are some of the things I think about when I am still awake, curled up against N.'s sleeping chest, listening to the irregular, syncopated breathing patterns of the house.

Another matriarch, this time my other great-grandmother—let's call her Cati—sailed here alone on a boat when she was sixteen. The trip took a few months. She didn't have any luggage. She had never stepped off land before, not even to swim. Within her first two days on board, she fell sick. She lost all her papers, everything she had saved to bring with her and start a new life. Her pocketbook fell overboard when she threw up.

A kind stranger she met at the port gave her the money to get from the port city to the cornfields, where others from her home country were waiting to offer her work. The stranger told her he would write down his name and address so that she could repay him when she was settled in. She watched the pen touch the paper to write it down for her. But when, sitting on the train with the ticket he had procured for her, she unfolded the piece of paper where he had written his information, it was blank.

Now you know that stranger was an angel! we say to one another.

Everyone in my family gets watery eyes when someone tells this story aloud. We're big on this kind of mythology.

But sometimes my mind gets hooked on other details. Like why she had a pocketbook in her hand while she was vomiting. A woman who knows enough to cross an ocean alone doesn't make this kind of mistake. I can't help my brain from worrying out the details, like whether an angel was the one to take all her papers from her, or if it was some other man.

The daughter of Cati is my grandmother Marie. She had ten children before the age of thirty-five, but before that she grew up with this story in a small house on Alexandra Street with two parents who preferred everything in the old country. She studied hard enough to get a scholarship to study chemistry at the prestigious local university. Her father told her she couldn't go because he heard that the university was full of communists.

My grandmother cried for days. She was two years older than her mother was when an angel on a ship either stole her pocketbook or saved her life. My grandmother's mother appealed to her husband, who appealed to the parish priest on her behalf.

The parish priest offered this counsel: If my grandmother agreed to say three Hail Marys for every credit hour she spent in class each week, she should be allowed to accept the scholarship.

I wonder how many of them she said. I would like to ask her, but she doesn't speak much anymore. She moves her mouth and starts sentences, but ever since she had a stroke, she can't get the words out. Her eyes do all the speaking—they house her irony, her frustration, her affection, her rage. Sometimes she gives a shrug of her shoulders that seems sheepish, but her eyes tell the other half of the story.

Now she sits with her chair angled toward the television when I visit. She keeps a rosary next to her remote control.

The day of the biopsy, I had been advised to take an aspirin prior to my arrival because the procedure had the potential to sting a little. We'll take a look under the microscope and see what's there before we start poking you, the doctor explained. Now, let your legs fall open. Scoot down a bit more.

I recoiled from the sound of the word *scoot*, the clamminess of his hands. I stared into the pulse of the fluorescent light as the doctor pushed the speculum inside me and said, Hmm, all right.

A nurse asked, How many should I prepare?

I'd like to take five, the doctor said.

The other nurse rubbed the side of my thigh and said, Just relax, honey.

Okay, here we go, announced the doctor. First one at two o'clock. You might feel a slight pinch.

Pain shot down the length of my legs. I winced.

Five o'clock, he said to the nurse.

I kept my eyes on the hands of the nurse rubbing my thigh.

Shh, sweetheart, you're doing great.

Eight o'clock sample coming next.

I tried to picture a round, flat-faced clock hanging in a classroom, to anticipate where the pain would come from, but

grandfather clocks and digital watches flooded my vision, dis-
orienting me.

Are you doing okay? someone asked.

Yes, I said, sensing it was the right answer.

Eleven o'clock.

Three o'clock.

When the doctor was finished, he left the room quickly, saying he'd let me get cleaned up, and the nurse gave me some gauze
and tissues and a pad. There was blood, and there was a vinegar
solution that they'd applied to stop the bleeding.

When the vinegar solution comes out, the doctor had explained
brightly before exiting the room, it'll just look like coffee grounds.

Coffee grounds, I'd repeated weakly.

Yep, the doctor had smiled. I only mention this so you're not
startled if you see something that looks like that in your underwear.

I walked out of the office clutching my gut. My underwear filled
with coffee grounds–like sediment that I had been instructed not
to let startle me. I had to be at work in an hour. I called my mother.

Where are you? she said.

I'm in the center of the city, walking toward the park.

Are there any stores around?

The *center* of the city, Mom, I said.

What do I know about that? said my mother sternly. What
stores do you see?

I looked around and answered honestly. I see Forever 21, I
said. Crate and Barrel. The Container Store. The Gap.

Perfect, says my mother. Walk into the Gap right now, pass
the registers and the sale items, look for the Gap Body section.
Do you see it?

I followed my mother's instructions. I entered the store, which appeared as if they were giving things away, the shelves were so disheveled. Yes, I said. I see it.

Good, said my mother. She talked me through each action with a quiet but persistent calm, like a voice teaching someone to disarm an explosive device set to detonate. My mother continued, There're always sales at this time of year. Underwear should be something like two for one, or buy two get one free, something like that, am I right?

I scanned the signs above the racks.

It's three pairs for the price of two, I said, nearing the display for underwear, pajamas, and exercise clothes.

Great, said my mother. A bargain. Buy three.

But I don't need three, I said. I don't even know how much all those biopsies cost.

My mother's voice spoke over mine, smoothing over my protest like a wrinkle in a tablecloth.

Listen, honey, buy three, she said. Three for two is a good deal. Put them on a credit card. It will give you peace of mind.

Within an hour of the biopsy, I stood at the front of a classroom and said to my students—while they were still my students—that the passive voice was to be avoided in this language that they were learning. That while it was a possibility that passive voice writing was considered eloquent, appropriate even, in their languages, inside this one it was viewed as a sign of weakness. That it was to be shunned.

Before entering the classroom, I'd followed my mother's instructions. I'd purchased the three pairs of underwear with a credit card. Then I walked past the registers in a cavernous old McDonald's without placing an order, located the bathrooms, and put all three of them on at once inside of my jeans. I emerged from the stall looking only slightly more bloated.

But listen to what you just said, my students said. Didn't you just use the passive voice? Are you sure you're a native speaker?

Of course I'm a native speaker, I said. I laughed, but it came out a little too loud and sharp, and I saw that it made the students skeptical.

The spoken and the written language are two entirely different realms, I advised them. What flies in one does not in the other and vice versa. It's the same in your native languages I'm sure.

The students had nodded uneasily, took notes in a mix of the language they were learning and the languages that were theirs.

Meanwhile, inside of my three pairs of underwear, small piles of soot resembling coffee grounds gathered in Rorschach-like patterns that I later studied, after class, when I was alone locked in a bathroom stall on the fifteenth floor of the building in the center of the city, as if trying to divine from their abstract forms some kind of narrative thread, as if they might augur what would come next.

It was ten o'clock on a Tuesday night when I emerged from the bathroom stall and walked the empty streets, the LCD screens lighting my way to the train with their suggestions of what could be bought to acquire more beauty, sex, and power—none of which meant anything to me at that time.

While an instructor of Language Elective for Non-Native Speakers, I compiled a short list of comments about the nature of people in this country that my students had made in their time here. Most of these were uttered without judgment, as if to spare my feelings, couched in the language of simple observation. Sometimes I take out my notes and read through my students' words, call to mind their voices. I wonder who is teaching them now, or if they are back in their countries, by choice or by force.

—People in this country begin many sentences with the word *I*.

—People in this country do not often embrace one another when they meet.

—People in this country prefer their own systems of measurement to universal systems.

—People here move their hands while speaking when angry or when giving directions. Otherwise, their hands are still.

When I was a child, we moved around a lot. My parents were working and going to school, but for several years when I was very young, my mom stayed home with me. I remember going to the mall often. I remember my mother pushing me in the stroller through racks and racks of clothes, a Frango mint nestled against the inside of my cheek like a secret.

When I was four years old, my grandmother Marie asked me, What is your address? Do you know where you live?

Yes, I answered confidently. Marshall Field's.

I'm not sure if I thought I was making a joke, or if I thought of the now-shuttered department store as a kind of second home. It was true that I spent many weekday afternoons getting pushed in the stroller under the welcoming green cursive-scrawled marquee. For my mother, the mall was a place of refuge: The power of shopping could connote a kind of reverence that was equal only to the power of prayer.

Before I lost my classes and my reproductive organs, before I started caring for R. every afternoon and dancing in bars every night, I spent my evenings going out with a series of different men I'd met on the Internet. I had been advised that by dating at a strategic rate, I would improve my chances of finding someone with whom I would want to combine my DNA before it was too late. To expedite the process, I used primarily two sites and sometimes a third, on which I posted photographs and answered multiple-choice questions that gave potential partners the answers to issues such as: my favorite positions during intercourse; my preferences on grooming etiquette for body hair; my spending habits; my typical use of and/or aversions to a potential partner's use of substances such as cigarettes, alcohol, weed, cocaine, amphetamines, etc.; my political beliefs, both publicly espoused and privately held.

That fall, when the doctor's phone calls started coming in, I had been primarily seeing two men. The first had retired at thirty-eight from a career as a hedge fund trader to pursue a doctorate in social psychology. His attitude toward substances was generally a bottle of wine a night and a smattering of cigarettes evenly spaced throughout the evening. His attitude toward body hair was anything goes. He was interested in a new career, in his words, championing social justice, but he was afraid to walk in my neighborhood at night, so we mostly slept at his place. The other man was an architect who specialized in biophilia, which he seemed aggravated he had to explain to me meant letting elements like plants and natural light back into design. His attitude toward substances was usually three cocktails and one joint per night. He had no body hair whatsoever, but mine didn't seem to startle him. He came from a rich family in a poor country, and he preferred not to sit in parks after sundown or to sit with his back to the door of the bar. They were both conventionally attractive and had attended prestigious universities situated not far from the city. I tried to remember which stories I had told one and which stories I had told the other so that I wouldn't repeat myself. I tried to rotate my nights with them to strategically delay the number of nights after which it would be necessary to accept their invitations to go home with them. I wouldn't mind going home with them, except for the fact that the experience was rarely enjoyable; you would think that with all the sex the men in the city were having, they would be better at having it, but for most of them I would record their performance in the C range: average engagement, demonstrates medial effort, with key areas in need of improvement.

N. has a membership to the art museum from back when he still considered himself a painter, and sometimes we go to see free films screened there at night. Once when we go to a film about refugee children who play with one another in a deserted border town and the guerrillas who watch out for them, N.'s eyes fill silently beside me in the theater, and I pretend not to notice. The subtitles of the film are necessary because the dialogue is in a language neither N. nor I understand. We leave the theater and stumble beneath nearby skyscrapers. We don't speak. I wonder how much of the story we were able to understand through the words that were printed for our benefit at the bottom of the screen in my language, and how much of the story is lost to us both.

Sometimes N. takes me to empty apartments between renovations that are not his but that he has keys to nevertheless.

I'm doing some work here, he says, so I've been sleeping here sometimes.

But there is no furniture.

Looking for the bathroom, I poke my head into one of the

bedrooms. There are several flattened moving boxes in a pile with a pillow on top.

N. is in what will become the living room waiting for me.

Ready? He smiles sincerely, his teeth showing, and I feel like I want to take him home.

Instead, we walk to the closest diner and tip the ceramic cups back into our mouths, wait for the chamomile to coat our throats and work its magic.

One night, we go on a long walk through a neighborhood that makes us think about tenement housing but that smells of ten-dollar gourmet tacos. We don't have the cash to pay any covers, but sometimes we like to walk without a destination in mind.

We get lost, and N. pauses in the middle of the street to consult his phone, turning it around in his hand looking for a point of orientation.

We can cross—he pauses, slowly sounding out a street name under his breath—and walk north.

A group of three women with a combination of very long hair and short skirts and very short hair and long skirts intentionally bump into N. while he is stopped on the sidewalk, giggling as they pass. Welcome to the city, honey, they say.

Tourists, they add, sizing me up as well.

N. and I smile at each other, meekly at first, like we know a pretty good joke that we aren't going to say aloud. Then the next thing we know, we are stopped there in the middle of the street, laughing so hard we couldn't move even if we'd wanted to. Cars honk at us, drivers yell obscenities. We laugh so hard our lungs hurt. My eyes start to tear so much I feel I have never laughed so hard before, and I lean up into N. and kiss him—quickly, almost imperceptibly—on his cheek, just above his perfect jawline.

Even later that night, I'm not sure what the joke was. But it has to do with geography and local intuition; it has to do with learned place names, how they can feel like loose cannons rolling around behind the uneven barrier of your teeth.

One of the cities is the one where N.'s mother eventually died. Another is the one where my mother still lives.

Why don't you come home? my mother says on the telephone every time I call. You can have your old room back. You can go jogging with your father in the evenings. You won't believe all the renovation downtown. Calliope Music is gone. There's a new sushi place there now. Sometimes we go there for dinner, and you won't believe that it's the chef from that Mongolian fusion place where you used to waitress. We'll go the next time you visit. When did you say that would be?

N.'s mother never calls.

When I ask him if he ever wants to return to the place where he was born, N. closes his eyes, like it is the stupidest question he has ever heard. N. never asks me if I want to go home, but for the record, the answer is no.

Later that night I find the book on a shelf in his bedroom.

I pick it up because I gravitate toward unfamiliar books among other people's personal property like insects toward the buzzing lights that electrocute them. It is the only book on his shelf, lodged between half-squeezed tubes of oil paint and a plastic snow globe enclosing a miniature replica of a city monument that looks like it was acquired in a tourist shop twenty years ago. I examine the slender book, published by Semicolon Press, its red, text-only cover and plain white font, written in N.'s language by the author Tomas Petritus. I can't stop myself from palming through pages, running my eyes over a few lines. As soon as I have my hands on it, I see N. shift.

What's this?

It's my mom's, N. says. It used to be my mom's.

I put the book down fast.

But later, after N. tells me a story (cousin, pistol), but before he tries—gently, unsuccessfully—to take off my clothes, he opens the book again. He starts to read aloud to me, just a few pages.

The next night, N. reads a little more. He reads; I listen. We continue like this every night we see each other until we make it through to the end one night.

Then we start over again, and, this time, I read it aloud to him as if it were written in my language.

LIST OF STUDENT OBSERVATIONS (CONT'D):

—People in this country have an interesting grasp of geography.

—People in this country open the spigot of the sink and let the water run full force while they wash the dishes.

—People in this country often smile showing as many teeth as possible at once.

—People in this country fill their carts at the supermarket as if preparing for a significant storm at any moment.

I was in the kitchen side of my studio apartment, preparing dinner, when the next round of doctors' calls reached me. The first call came from the office of an oncologist east of the park.

The nurse asked to speak to me and told me my doctor had referred me there. That I should come in as soon as possible. Tomorrow, ideally. They would create a space for me.

The following afternoon, the oncologist greeted me in the company of four residents and two nurses. He spoke theatrically, waving his arms around, drawing pictures of cell growth that were ostensibly for my benefit, but I saw every medical student in the room taking notes, so I couldn't be sure if the detail of the drawing was more on account of their lesson or due to the magnitude of my body's failure.

When he paused to entertain my questions, I asked: Is this cancer or precancer?

The oncologist paused, pursed his lips as if he'd just tasted something sour. Language, he said. Let's start by getting the language right.

I nodded.

Cancer is a layman's term, he said. It doesn't mean anything for our purposes here.

One of the medical students had kind eyes. My eyes met his as I searched for the correct words to ask my question again, and he looked away, demurred.

Adenocarcinoma in situ? I said instead.

The oncologist nodded, pleased I had come prepared with vocabulary that wouldn't waste his time.

He said, I don't even know how your doctor found it, but it's there. We're going to remove a part of it to study it. It's technically a surgical procedure, but I'd like to encourage you to think of it as a large single biopsy. In theory it's a procedure that is both therapeutic and diagnostic.

The students took furious notes and kept looking only at my paper gown–clad shoulders, not my eyes.

Whenever N. and I find each other out at night, one of two things occurs. If we run into one another early in the evening, we say hello and watch each other dance with everyone else in the room—noticing strangers' arms on each other's hips and shoulders all night—before finding one another again just before the bar closes. Then we dance all the remaining songs together, sloppily, happily, our feet dragging through the steps. The alternative is that one of us arrives earlier than the other, or we don't cross paths until the very end of the evening. When we both have given up on the thought of seeing each other, we instead give ourselves over to the music, to the crowd: We dance with everyone, we sing all the songs quietly, under our breath. This is also not a bad way to spend a night. But whenever I am in such a state—say it's around midnight, and suddenly I catch N.'s eye while I'm in another dance—I walk directly to him, or he walks directly to me, as soon as the song ends. We smile. He offers me his hand, and I take it in mine.

When I dance, it is as if there is nothing that exists outside of the rhythm of a measure of music. I can feel all the anxiety drain from my muscles because there are no options to analyze, no choices to make. Sometimes, with the beat of the music, I step forward into the empty space N.'s body creates for me. Other times, the same foot rocks back as N.'s body pushes closer into mine. The symmetry of the steps overrides any turns or leads. N. could throw my body into a series of spins or circle his own body around mine; he could set me free for several beats or pick up my wrist with the opposite hand, and I would always complete the measure with a rock step, backward then forward, that feels safe as a homecoming.

Invariably someone comes up to me at the end of the night: a woman who is sitting at the bar drinking wine or at a table with her friends, who just came after work for a few drinks and stayed, or who is only there to listen to the music. The woman always says, I came over to say how much I loved watching you two dance together. And I see that in this woman's mind, N. and I have spent our entire lives dancing together, that we are deeply committed to one another, and our desire emanates from our hips and elbows and arms as we circle around each other's bodies. I always smile and I say, Oh, thanks a lot. I am capable of separating truths in my mind, so on the one hand, it's a source of great comfort to know we inspire strangers to come to this conclusion. Because there is no time I feel more at home in my own body than when I dance with N. And so the fact that N. and I only ever tell each other half the truth of our stories, or that I never know when N. and I will see each other until the instant he appears, or that I have no idea where N. sleeps on the nights that I am not with him is irrelevant.

There is a period of time during these months when time stops. I live outside of ambition.

I pick up R. from school, and if it is Monday, Wednesday, or Friday, I take him to physical therapy and read in the waiting room with the other caretakers. If it is Tuesday or Thursday, I take him to visit the speech pathologist. Through the one-way observation window in the waiting room, I see R. sitting cross-legged on a pillow on the floor across from her. Through the window, I hear R. willing his mouth to make the sounds requested of him by the cardboard cut-out letters that the speech pathologist holds up one at a time. Sometimes, when R. gets frustrated by the difficulty of trying to pronounce a letter, he picks up a letter's form with great intentionality, as if he only needs to get a better look at it, and then throws it against the wall.

How did he do today? I ask the speech pathologist when R.'s forty-five minutes have ended.

The speech pathologist is positive to a fault, but I see that it is because she has deep faith in R.'s abilities to improve.

Excellent, she says. Or, other times: Today he's tired, but he still did great.

Well, should we get out of here? I always ask R. once his

session has ended. And sometimes he says in a low voice, No, no, no. He throws his arms around the speech pathologist, as if he has a lot more energy to give to her exercises. Other times, he signs the word *yes* and hugs me just as fiercely.

After dinner and his bath, I read with R. beside him in his bed. He often wants to hear the same stories over and over again, and I try to sneak a new one into the repertoire. Aside from books about wild animals trapped in cities, he is also drawn to stories that fall into one of the following categories: mistakes and blunders, machines on the run, metamorphoses, and feasts.

Sometimes when I point to words, he sounds them out himself, and sometimes he makes me do all the work.

At night, the pattern repeats itself with N. I read aloud and he listens. Whenever we read together, I focus on the mothers' feelings of loss as they register in their bodies; N. focuses on their militancy and ability to organize. I focus on the narrator as an outsider, his elaborate field notes. N. focuses on the rising intensity of the threats the mothers receive. I think it's okay that we have different points of entry into this world. I think it's okay that a book can mean different things for different readers.

Occasionally, when I read aloud in my own language, finding words of mine to replace the words in the book, N. argues with me about their meaning, but mostly he trusts me with my language, and I trust him with his.

A few times, I see a kind of fierceness in N. Each time it surprises me, but it passes quickly. The first time, a stranger places his hand on N.'s shoulder in the bar, and N. swings around so quickly to face him that I see the man put his hands up in defense.

Whoa, slow down, says the man. I think that's my jacket, that's all, the man says, gesturing to the black leather heap folded over N.'s arm.

N. lifts the jacket by the scruff like an animal cub and studies its label.

Sorry, man, he says, my mistake.

He hands the jacket over and shrugs. The man gives a half smile and retreats quickly with the jacket.

Another time, N. and I are back at the museum. There's a collection of photographs on migrations. We walk slowly through the faces of children in the arms of their mothers in inflatable boats, young men walking through the desert alone, an old woman in line at a border crossing while an official towers over her with a document in his hand. We walk side by side between the photographs, sometimes remarking on the origin of an artist or a use of light or color.

Later, I ask N. how it feels to be alone in a country that is not his.

I am not alone here, he snaps. I have people here, same as you.

Oh, sorry, I say. I never heard you talk about anyone here.

I mean, it turns out they don't want anything to do with me, N. says. But I didn't come here chasing some ambiguous dream. I came here because I have family here.

I wait for him to say more, but the line of his brow hardens. He quickens his pace and says nothing.

It is the beginning of December when, in a town not far from the city, a boy of fourteen is shot by the police and left to die on the sidewalk. His skin is black, his hands are in his pockets, his head shifts quickly to the left just after the officer said no sudden movements. Always different variations on the same story. When the news breaks, N. and I are sitting on a park bench after dancing but before getting kicked out by the cops, my head nestled into the crook of his neck.

We agree to meet the next day in the city center with posterboard and black markers. We take turns using one another's backs, covered in down coats, as steady surfaces to write on the posterboard: on one side in N.'s language and on the other in mine. As we walk through the streets with so many of the people of our city who are tired, more tired than N. and I can even imagine, we take turns holding the homemade sign high above our heads. We flip it from front to back, back to front, methodically, offering the message first in one language, then in the other, as if searching for a channel with good reception.

When the woman with the megaphone at the front leads us through the doors of a department store, into a giant mall, we surround her and march inside. We all lie down in the giant atrium of the mall in front of an enormous Christmas tree covered in lights and golden ornaments. We are pretending to be dead, but with our eyes open. I am an outsider who has been living in the neighborhood of the woman with the megaphone for a decade. But I cannot ignore the fact that this will never be my neighborhood, that I am a transplant who comes with her own history. So I lie dead with my eyes open; I consent to follow the instructions of the woman with the megaphone. She sings out to us on the floor, and we respond.

I am on the periphery of the group, and out of the corner of my eye I can see a woman in her sixties with blond hair and a trench coat.

People are just trying to do their Christmas shopping, she's saying, shaking her head. Then she starts to yell it.

People are just trying to live their lives without getting murdered by the white supremacist state, patiently responds the woman with the megaphone.

It's Christmas! says the woman. She looks like she is on the verge of tears.

Though my mother is not blond—in fact, she has a headful of thick black curls that sometimes causes her to be mistaken for a foreigner—there is something about the woman that reminds me of my mother. I feel a prickling sensation at the back of my eyes as I think about my mother Christmas shopping in the strip malls in the cornfields, wanting at once to be shopping with her and to be playing dead on the floor of this mall far away from the place where I was born.

A Muzak version of "God Rest Ye Merry, Gentlemen" plays softly from somewhere, and I feel a wave of nostalgia for the department stores and cornfields pass over me.

I am playing dead with the crowd at the request of the woman with the megaphone as an act of protest, to reject the hypocrisy that places arbitrary value on our individual bodies, but there is a deeper part of me, lying prostrate in the mall's atrium, that feels myself cry out in surrender: to the architecture of the glowing signage of each unique store, to the inevitably pristine white surface of the walls that grow toward the ornamental design of the skylights. I can't help but feel insignificant in the context of this exalted space. I look around at the bodies on the floor with me, our dark skin and our light skin, our boniness and our girth, our secondary sex characteristics masked by our puffy winter coats and windbreakers and denim jackets unfit for the snow and wind of the city. I feel let down by the promise of these grand commercial spaces, the feeling of security they offered me as a child walking them with my mother. The thought washes over me that playing dead here is only an exhibit of the obvious and inevitable.

N.'s mittened hand is within reach, and I grab it. He squeezes my hand, once, twice, three times, like a code. I don't know how to interpret it, but I feel grateful that he is there beside me, with all the other bodies piled on the floor, gazing up at all the twinkling ornaments of the mall's atrium.

A few weeks later, I drive home for Christmas. My family gathers around a tree to sing Christmas carols. The older generations prefer songs with religious significance, while the children clamor for any songs that make reference to Santa, presents, reindeer, being "good." For this reason, we alternate between the two genres, a commercial Christmas song for every two holy ones.

When I was a child, my uncle would play all the songs on the acoustic guitar and we would sing the lyrics as memory allowed, until someone made homemade photocopies of the lyrics of our favorite songs, which were passed around every year.

Now, we've gotten ahold of a DVD that can be cued to each song through an organized table of contents. We select the song we want to sing, and the music starts up with the tinny notes of synthesizers. A blue screen appears, on top of which the lyrics of the song are projected. A bouncing white ball hovers over each syllable when it is the correct moment to belt it out. Perhaps we exchange fewer glances with one another across the room, as our eyes are trained on the white bouncing ball. We sing loudly, joyfully, our minds swimming with shopping lists; we sing wistfully, our thoughts catching on unfulfilled desires or memories of those who are no longer with us. All our faces are illuminated by the blue glow of the television.

LIST OF STUDENT OBSERVATIONS (CONT'D):

—People in this country are not often shy.

—People in this country are not obligated to vote in local, state, or national elections.

—People in this country keep the rooms so cold that they have to wear sweaters in the heat of summer.

—People in this country like to give advice.

When the oncologists and the medical students and the nurses informed me that a radical intervention was necessary, I nodded vigorously without speaking. I continued to nod at the scheduling desk, in the elevator, out the revolving door, and down the street. When I reached the edge of the street I broke into a run toward the park. The park was large enough to swallow someone whole, but I didn't run long. I am not a runner. I ran to the first soft patch of grass in the shade. I dove headfirst into it. I cried for me and for my mother and for my grandmother, and for my great-grandmother—and I cried about how in some other languages there are words for concepts like great-great-grandmother that don't exist in mine. And I felt I had failed, derailed this chain of women—all of whom were tougher, all of whom had less with which to make things work.

It was 1 p.m. in the city. It was lunch hour in a neighborhood that is now a mix of rich people and poor people. None of the rich people or the poor people stopped to ask if I was okay, to see if I was breathing, to inquire if I needed help, as I continued to heave face down and inhale mouthfuls of grass and dirt.

A̲ll of this happened nine months before I met N., but I tell him none of it. It is another story without a gun, without a man, without a steep plot arc or a clear payoff, so I keep the story to myself.

Sometimes, N. says, I want to be closer to you. He shifts into me in the bed, loops the gold filigree of my necklace several times around his index finger.

But I only smile one of my grandmother Marie's complex multi-layered smiles, twitch my fingers in my lap as if moving them through rosary beads, one by one.

Close enough, I think.

There is one more matriarch I can count. I know her only as a photograph. Let's call her Clora. She has hard lines around her mouth, and she wears the practical gold jewelry of a woman who keeps all of her most valuable assets on her body at all times.

She is the end of the line, as far back as I can trace. I know absolutely nothing about her except for the city where she was born, the name of the man she married, and the names of the children she gave birth to—my great-grandmother among them.

I hang her photograph on the wall above my desk. I don't want to say that I pray to her because that's not exactly accurate. I spend a lot of time studying the creases of her face and thinking the word *please.*

When I woke up, groggy and drugged, in a public hospital in the city center, my mother was there. She had driven fifteen hours to help me with the recovery from the surgery. She sat in the waiting room with a little plastic bag full of tissues and another plastic bag full of raisins. She must have packed them ahead of time, in the house where I grew up and where she still lives, and carried them with her across the country and into the waiting room. All that week, my mother slept next to me in the bed of my studio apartment and made all my meals, even though she didn't understand where I went grocery shopping in my neighborhood, in stores where half the packaging is printed in other languages. My mother grew up in the neighborhoods of immigrants, but these are languages she doesn't understand. I didn't know how to talk to her all that week, because I didn't know how to talk to anyone. I felt alone, very alone, too alone to acknowledge the presence of anyone outside my body, even the person inside whose body I had once lived.

We lay side by side in my bed at night, and I told my mom stories, which were actually just paraphrased lines from Wikipedia entries on topics like *hysteria (female)* and *sterilization (compul-*

sory, history of) that I'd started memorizing while on heavy doses of pain medication.

To this, my mom said, Hush. In the case of my body, the biopsy had revealed malignant growths; I was armed with every ounce of possible information and signed the waiver form for the removal of the diseased organs with my own hand. My mother reminded me of these things as she pulled me out of the shower every time I sat down while the water drained out beneath me, and wrapped my naked arms in a bath towel.

Sometimes when I think back on that week with my mother, I get confused. I wonder if this was something my mother did to take care of me, or if it's something that the other mothers did to take care of Sofia or Lexus or Queenie. I wonder if I read their stories so many times I migrated pieces of them into my own memories. Or if this is actually just the kind of thing that all mothers do.

The last time I see N., we end up at his apartment, the real apartment, with furniture and the old couple who sigh in their sleep in the living room. That night, I am reading aloud to N., and abruptly, he asks me to stop.

When he asks me to stop reading, Queenie has just asked Petritus to stop talking to Zara. We are almost to the chapter break, but N. stops me, says he doesn't want to hear any more. We are lying side by side, on the couch that is his bed, against which are propped the last canvases he hasn't touched for over a year, which are full of slick dark paint that looks like a mix of dirt and blood or oil.

I place the book on the shelf above our heads and reach to turn off the light. N.'s hand intercepts mine.

I'm not tired, N. says. I just don't want to read.

What do you want to do? I ask him.

N. pauses and looks briefly at the ceiling.

What are you doing here? he says.

Reading with you, I say.

What are you getting out of it? he asks.

You mean as a reader? I say. Or as a person?

I mean, why do you care? It has nothing to do with your life.

So I should only care about stories that relate directly to my life? I say.

Forget it.

What's wrong? I say.

N. shakes his head, goes quiet. Then he says, I guess we're never going to sleep together.

Maybe I should go, I say.

Never mind, N. says. Forget it.

He weaves his arm around my waist, pulls me closer to him, as we always sleep. I start to drift off quickly. I feel like it's the middle of the night, like I've been asleep for several hours already, when I feel the pressure of N.'s body over mine. I feel his breath on my cheek and the cool, sandpapery grip of his hands pushing mine down into the bed.

My thoughts become someone else's. I freeze. I stare at one of his unfinished paintings—long red streaks that fall like rain through the foreground of a darkened metropolis—and think about how beneath the part of me that feels it cannot move, there is another part that understands: I am not in danger, he will let go, and that part doesn't feel pain or anger, it just feels very, very tired. How as soon as he lets go, I'll gather my things and leave this apartment. He makes no attempt to remove my clothes. Our eyes meet. His lips brush against my own, once, twice. His grip tightens then loosens from my hands, and I feel them begin to throb. His eyes don't look angry; they look like they're trying to formulate a question. I look at him not with disgust, but with all the exhaustion accumulated inside me. Finally, he lets go. But when he does, I don't move to gather my things. I don't sit up in bed. I stare at him for several seconds more, until N. looks away, turns to face the wall. I think of the middle-aged woman who sighs in her bed on the other side of this door, and the man who holds her in her sleep. I don't want to walk past her, as if suddenly, my presence in her home has become sordid. I don't want to risk waking her up.

Instead, I start to cry, silently, but my body shakes uncontrollably, my breathing becomes labored. Shh, N. says, shh. He places one arm around my shoulders. With the other, he is stroking my hair like a mother. The longer I allow myself to be comforted by N., the more I realize I don't want to go home. I don't want to cross by the sleeping woman in the living room. So I stay, and we fall asleep side by side. We don't speak of what happened.

But in the morning, the feeling of N.'s weight stays with me. I can still detect a heaviness in my chest. And while N. is in the bathroom brushing his teeth and pushing his only leather belt through the loops of his jeans, I take Petritus's book off his shelf and shove it deep into the belly of my bag. And only later, after N. has walked me to the train, and after he has taken me to the bakery on the corner and asked for several pastries that he handed to me in a greasy waxed-paper bag, do I position my face directly in front of his and say to him, Why?

N.'s eyes look wet, and he blinks away whatever is there just as the train pulls up. I board the train before N. opens his mouth to give me his answer. The book weighs down my right shoulder. The automatic doors close between us. He stands on the platform, and I stand on the train. His eyes remain on mine until we pull away from the station. My throat is dry, the taste of shame pooling behind my senses. I think, I hate N. more than I have ever hated anyone, and at the same time he is the only one capable of comforting me. I continue to stand as the train pulls away, and I keep my gaze trained on the skyline. As I watch the city from the train, the skyscrapers sparkle in the distance, and I feel separate from this place, removed, looking down from above, like I am passing temporarily through a strange land to which I do not belong.

II

II

FIELD NOTES

October 24

The mothers grow exhausted by the growing lists of hypothetical scenarios. They continue to meet for the regular reasons, but also, they start to make phone calls. They start to make posters. They board buses with laminated photos of the missing persons who are their sons hanging from lanyards around their necks. When they arrive in larger towns and cities, they spend entire afternoons standing in the public squares that border key state and municipal buildings.

State and municipal officials and authorities regret to inform the mothers that they won't have an opportunity to listen to the stories they have come to tell.

Instead, when they return home empty-handed, the mothers take turns telling their stories to Madame O, whose real name is Carlotta, who sits with her tarot pack and gems lined up on a card table in the central square. She shifts their palms around inside her own, looking for clues, concludes their lifelines are long or short or of average length. She can't tell them anything about those of their sons without their sons' palms present, she explains. The mothers nod, shift around uncomfortably in their lawn chairs. It's like the opposite of saying a burial can't take place without a body. Madame O understands better than most because she's already buried three of her own.

They take turns telling their stories to the empty confessional box where they imagine a man of the church sits and offers guidance in a steady voice. The Sisters of Our Holy Ghost are not qualified for this kind of work; they stick to humming out the standard litanies and orations at vespers. So the mothers speak to themselves inside the box. They speak aloud the same stories that run though their heads on a constant loop. Then they assign themselves recitations of prayers, a kind of penance without atonement. Somewhere around three consecutive Hail Marys is the standard length of time they can keep a clear head. Or they sit inside the box and rock back and forth.

They take turns telling their stories to the psychologists who are bused in for an afternoon every other month for group therapy.

They take turns telling their stories to the traveling board of rotating officials who represent the Commission of the Truth.

They take turns telling their stories to me.

With few exceptions, they withhold nothing from me. I record everything they say. They never ask me why I am interested in their stories. They never ask what I will do with their stories once I have finished documenting them and transcribing my notes into a publication of my findings. Nine out of ten mothers are so tired of not being listened to, they will talk to anyone who asks for their story, no questions asked.

October 30

They start to work in the capital. As maids, as housekeepers, as nannies. Or they work in cafeterias, in street markets, on assembly lines. Some of them bus in and out every day. Some of them are gone for weeks at a time and send money home for their children until they can afford an alternative.

Mimi walks around nearby towns all morning selling fruit out of a wheelbarrow.

Lexus stands on the same streets at night offering sex to people in passing cars.

Lira sews and tailors clothes. Also, she collects bottles and cans.

Eli bakes pastries and loads them into the backpack that used to belong to her son. Then she hikes to the bus station to sell the pastries to passengers. She boards the idling buses, walking up and down the aisles between the rows of seats, before they depart.

There are different strategies. One is to tell one's story, which is to say, how one came to be a person who survives on selling pastries on idling buses.

She started out like that: key facts, broad strokes.

Yeah, I'll take a pastry, a fat man with a cigarette tucked behind his ear said after she finished her pitch, calling her to him with his hand. While Eli undid the zipper of her son's backpack walking toward him, he slid his foot out into the aisle so it made contact with her ankle, knocking her off balance. As she tried to right herself, the man pretended to help brace her fall, pushing his two hands into her breasts.

Nothing that came next mattered: how she heard her own voice move from a mutter to shouting *son of a bitch*, how the bus driver started making his way toward her to escort her roughly back down the aisle; how the man with the cigarette stared out his window like a bystander more interested in a stray dog stretching its belly up on the sidewalk; how a woman's heeled shoe twitched nervously in her peripheral vision.

It was later, at home, lying awake, repeating the name of her town at the ceiling—just as she'd said it aloud to the passengers—when she saw her mother floating face down in the river there, that she started to shiver and ball up fingers into fists that she flung into everything in the room. She doesn't tell this story anymore.

Eli's new story goes like this:

Ladies and gentlemen, pastries for sale! Homemade, baked with care, baked with the best local ingredients! Get them while they're fresh! Get them while they're hot!

The days she wears lipstick she sells out by noon.

November 10

This morning, in the capital, as I transcribed the latest batch of tapes into my notebook, the following notice was passed under the door of the apartment where I am staying. My long days here have been rather isolating, so I ran quickly to the door to receive the letter:

Attention: Sirs, Residents of the Tower

Cordial greetings,

This is to inform you that we have received complaints from the residents of the lower apartments, because objects have been falling from the higher apartments, including items such as: hairs, eggs, papers, cigarette butts, pastry wrappers, liquids, etc., which in addition to generating inconveniences, can cause harm and personal injury to those enjoying their private spaces.

Due to the above, we ask that you transmit this notice to the other members of your household in order to achieve a healthy coexistence in this unit.

We appreciate the attention and cooperation of all.

Sincerely,
The Administration

I have spent much time transcribing these notes on my balcony, but I have never seen any of the named objects drop in the nearby air. It's true that I inhabit one of the upper apartments, so the possibility exists that the culprits reside in one of the units that are between mine and the lower apartments.

What I have witnessed from my own balcony is items ascending, items such as: barbecue smoke, cigarette smoke, kites, dog fur, the sounds of cries and cannonball splashes from the pool, helium balloons with messages like *You're special!* and *Happy birthday princess!*

Farther out, higher up still, over the temporary homes of the internal alien settlements, vultures ascend and descend.

Swoop, climb, dive.

One imagines that these flight paths, too, enact personal injury and inconvenience in the private spaces of residents who have settled there.

For decades, local officials favored forcibly removing the settlements from the surrounding mountains. The reason most often given is that the settlements are eyesores, and moreover, they are illegally constructed with found materials by individuals who lack proper state identification.

Now, there's a more popular strategy for dealing with the torrent of internal aliens who arrive in the capital: The mayor is building them libraries. Nothing like a good book to take your mind off the systematic loss of everything you once held dear. International architects show up with blueprints for state-of-the-art constructions; the libraries win prizes, they're so beautiful and sustainably designed. As the neighborhoods are slowly beginning to change, and their storied violence becomes enshrined in legends sold by the state tourism industry, the municipal authorities have adopted this new strategy. Rather than destroy the settlements, the capital has begun to invest in them: The libraries are soon accompanied by infrastructure, parks, murals, the works. Now there are companies offering guided tours up there in the periphery of the city. For a modest price, you can enter their makeshift communities (*by day, of course*, the guidebooks assert, *it's 100 percent safe*). The excuse of visiting newly minted, heavily policed cultural landmarks offers the opportunity to marvel at the ingenuity with which internal alien communities survive. Sometimes, you can see their chickens in the yards, their clothes lying out to dry flat on the roofs. Their houses are built from the most unlikely materials—plastic tarps, corrugated sheet metal, cardboard, plastic bottles, tin cans.

November 16

The women—in both the capital and the small villages—are rumored to be among the most beautiful in the world, in terms of basic principles of aesthetics. It's all about classic ratios.

Think eyes to nose to mouth; hips to waist to breasts.

Surgically modifying physical characteristics in compliance with such ratios is always a possibility. There are different types of pricing plans. Better doctors, lower risks of infection, depending on your income, your neighborhood. But the point is, there are always options.

Queenie does not conform to any of these ratios. In short: Her hair is a wild shock of curl, cropped around her ears. Her breasts are the size of a girl's. Her right leg is a prosthetic. It would be considered ethically questionable to provide further commentary on the physical makeup of one of my informants, so I will admit that I often find it refreshing to cross paths with her and leave it at that.

Besides, Queenie is not technically an informant because she never signed the waiver to be interviewed on record.

The second time I saw her was at a birthday party where I had been invited by some of the other mothers. I had the release forms and the recording device in my backpack. I wouldn't normally pull out all the interview apparatus at a birthday party, but I had gotten permission from my hosts to do a little light questioning.

Queenie looked at the empty line by the X of the release form I produced. She stuck her long fingernail into the white space there and dragged it until the space became a tear clear to the other side.

What are you doing? I asked her.

Letting some air in, she said.

I watched her walk away with her slow but graceful limp. As she did, I noticed the parts of her T-shirt where the sweat had made the color of the fabric darker. She walked to the corner of the yard where an old man was standing behind a speaker hooked up to his phone. She whispered something in his ear, and he nodded as he cued the next song. Everyone broke into cheers when the first chords sounded—a local favorite. The refrain lists the names of nearby rivers.

Queenie kept the beat in her wrists, drummed her fingers across her thighs. She watched the crowd and danced with no one. After a few minutes Zara walked up to her mother. Queenie wrapped her arms around the girl, and the two started to sway very slowly, as if listening to a song that shares no discernible characteristics with the one that everyone else hears.

It was later that day at the birthday party that Zara cornered me. The sun had gone down long before, but the music was still going. Everyone was dancing in a circle around the birthday girl. I was standing under an olive tree in the corner of the yard, taking down observations in my notebook, when I noticed Zara coming toward me with a soda that she uncapped and placed in my hand.

Lemon, she shrugged. That's all that's left.

Lemon's good, I said.

Zara rolled her eyes.

See that girl over there? she said.

Which one? I asked. There was nothing but girls left in the yard.

The fat one, said Zara. The one that can't dance.

I nodded.

It's a friend of her uncle, she said. He's the one who promised jobs to all the boys that are missing.

Oh? I said. I took a swig of my soda.

Zara said, Maybe you want to write that down in your little notebook.

I said nothing.

We stood side by side without speaking for a few minutes, watching the girls dance.

My brother's gone, she said then. Did you figure that out yet?

No, I said softly. I didn't know.

I held out my hand to her, offering it as a gesture of comfort, but she grabbed it and shook it instead.

Zara, I said. I'm very sorry to hear that.

Listen, she said. She shook her head and thinned her lips before she spoke. Let's make a deal, okay? Quid pro quo.

Excuse me? I asked.

It's Latin, she explained.

I know that, I said. Why do you?

School, she shrugged.

We both heard Queenie's voice then, calling out her name from the kitchen: Zara! We made ourselves silent in the shadows of the trees until she went back inside.

You never saw me here, Zara said, pushing a piece of paper into my hand.

I waited until later that night to unfold the note in my pocket.

Meet me tomorrow after school, in the square.
Bring your recording device.

November 17

The square was still quiet when I arrived, just before school let out. I sat and waited for several minutes on the same bench. Slowly, the regular packs of uniformed girls started to fill the space with their talk. I waited until I could pick Zara out from the rest of the group, as she wandered off by herself, and I watched her walk up to me.

Oh, hi, she said. You came.

Hi, Zara, I said.

She gave me her best fake smile. She said, I know I'm not exactly your top choice interview, but my mother wouldn't talk to you for anything in the world, so maybe you'll make an exception.

I'm not sure I understand, I said.

Do you want to know what happened to my brother? she asked.

I blinked. I would like to hear your story if you would like to share it with me, I said.

Zara nodded, Okay, yeah, that's what I thought. Do you want me to tell you what the quo is now or later?

The quo? I said.

The thing that I want in return for my story.

I shrugged. Zara—

It would be nothing for you, she said. It's just my bike. It has a busted wheel.

I nodded. I would be happy to help you, regardless of whether you tell me your story.

Okay, she said. You better turn that thing on because I'm about to start.

She paused for a second, stared at me hard until I looked away. Then she closed her eyes for a good twenty seconds, and her voice wandered off to a different place because it came out even softer than usual when she started to speak:

The bike was my brother's. It had wide handlebars that fit me sitting between them perfectly. I never had my own bike, but it didn't matter because we mostly wanted to go to all the same places anyway. Anderson is a better pedaler because he's three years older, and I lean back on my elbows and steer us by shifting my weight around. We could go really fast this way. We got good at it. Sometimes we raced cars. Nothing feels better than winning a race with a car. Even if the car doesn't know it's a race.

The day I came out of school and his bike wasn't where we left it, I waited around for a while, but he never showed up, so I started walking home alone. Later, on my way, I found the bike in a ditch with the front wheel bent in half. It was really hard to push home with just the one working wheel. When my mom saw me with the bike and without Anderson, she ran out of the house and told me not to leave until she got back. She came home very late. I watched her from the window of the kitchen, walking slowly up the hill, holding her forehead inside her hand. She tried to blink the wet from her eyes when she saw me there in the kitchen waiting up for her. Then she said that no one knew where Anderson was and that there were going to be a lot of new rules in our house.

Zara continued to speak without waiting for any of my questions. I nodded to encourage her to go on, but her eyes, when they opened at all, stayed trained toward my hands, on the red light beside the word RECORD:

Anderson is still Anderson when I see him in the middle of the night in dreams, and he's always mad about the busted wheel. He kicks the side of the mattress with his foot and says all the words that our mom would never let him say inside the house, in one breath. And I say, Who cares about the wheel? Where are you? He never says. Sometimes he shrugs like he's not even sure.

I've gotten used to walking everywhere again. It takes a lot longer, but sometimes I don't even notice because my mind starts moving all over the place like crazy, I don't even try to control it. Some people say to me that my brother got killed for being a traitor. At first, I wondered if that could be true. But then I think: 1) My brother would have told me if he was a traitor, because we tell each other everything, and 2) Anderson is twelve, he's just a kid.

Now I've stopped listening to what people say. Sometimes I get in fights and get sent home from school. Sometimes I just stare into space and pretend that I can't hear anyone. In my brain I turn everyone into another species, and they become little insects that speak some spider or cockroach language I don't understand. Kids can say whatever they want, and it doesn't matter. I know who is finding the boys to send away, because I saw the way he was talking to my brother a few days before, and my brother is not the only one he talked to, and I am not the only one who has seen him around. He's not from here. He's threatening people to keep them from talking, but there's no one here who doesn't know what's going on. He's a stranger here, like you, so he had to make contacts. I don't know his name, but he's staying with Clarice's family and has been for a while. See Clarice over there, the fat girl from yesterday? Now she's in front of the cathedral, talking with two other girls, and now she's cupping her hand around her mouth to whisper something about me to Anaïs, that idiot, and now she's laughing. I couldn't care less. I'm only telling you all this so you can include it in your report. People are watching you, I guess you figured that out. But as long as you're still here, you could listen to what I'm saying and you could write th—

    End of tape.

Are you threatening me? I asked Zara, my index finger heavy on the STOP button.

    No, she said. I thought you knew you were being watched. Why do you think my mother doesn't want me to talk to you?

November 20

In the mall closest to my living tower, there is a popular arcade that features a wave-making machine. Imagine surfing, right here in the middle of the mountains, with the help of highly specialized eyewear and a video of the sea that runs on a constant loop. Virtual pelicans circle and search for fish—background details, little touches to make the experience feel more real.

The waves are large but mostly peaceful. They crest and fall, crest and fall.

All without passing through coastal areas of the country that lack infrastructure and are subject to routine violence.

All without breathing in mouthfuls of salt.

Keeping balance amid the virtual waves is not as easy as it looks. If you fall from your board, the waves appear to grow in size—the shore shrinks in the distance. The degree of panic one can feel alone in the darkened room during such incidents is testament to the accuracy of the illusion.

I visited the arcade today with a fistful of coins. Since returning to the capital, I think often of Zara; of the missing boys; of the value of documentation; of how exhausted I am of asking every-one to testify.

When I fell hard from my surfboard, the room went completely dark around me, imitating the ocean. The virtual waves crashed over my head. All I could see was the black water. I grasped for my board, but it was gone. I treaded water until I watched my life points slowly peter out. I was still gasping for breath when I pulled back the curtain and exited the arcade.

I sat on a bench beneath a synthetic palm tree in the mall's large central corridor for a few minutes to catch my breath. After I recovered, leaning onto the railing overlooking the atrium, I noticed the children pedaling below in patient circles around the indoor track. The children were between five and ten years old, and they each had their own bicycle or scooter. Their parents stood by in the nearby observation deck and shouted words of encouragement. My gaze rested firm on a little girl with a pony-tail as I started my descent on the escalator. I glided past the food court into the belly of the mall's first floor. It didn't take me long to locate the bike shop, where I waited in line to be attended to.

Fifteen minutes later, I left with a tire, a wheel, and a hex wrench that would allow me to lower the seat of a boy's bike so a girl could reach its pedals.

November 27

When I returned to my research site the following week, I chose an hour that I suspected Queenie would be at the bus terminal with Eli, selling pastries, to knock on the door of her home with the wheel in my hand.

Zara answered. Her eyes locked onto the wheel and didn't deviate.

I'm not allowed to talk to you anymore, she said to the wheel.

We don't have to talk, I said. Just let me in to work on the bike.

She stepped back from the door like she wasn't going to intervene, but she wasn't saying she approved either.

Within twenty minutes, it was a functioning bike again. We didn't talk. I tapped my hand on the seat as an invitation for her to take it for a spin. She didn't know how to ride, so we worked on it. I gave her a push to get started. She fell a few times before she got the hang of things. She learned to lean to one side to brake. When Queenie came home from the station with her backpack half-full of unsold pastries, Zara was riding in circles around the street. Queenie had a light look on her face for a second, as if she'd witnessed some divine act of grace, before her eyes settled on me and her face contorted into a scowl.

Do you have kids? Queenie asked me.

I shook my head. I've dedicated my life to my research.

So I see, she said, before walking inside and closing the door firmly behind her.

December 3

A few TV cameras showed up in front of state and municipal buildings to record the spaces the mothers occupy with their laminated photos on lanyards around their necks, the spaces where the mothers have been transformed into monsters, pariahs, enemies of the state. The mothers have become legendary for the speed with which they have attracted the attention of state and municipal authorities. It must be some kind of a record.

Behind closed doors, and occasionally to their faces, the mothers have been called: hags, old bags, liars, fools, whores, beggars, prostitutes, peasants, undesirables, scum.

Inventors of histrionics, hysterics, public unrest.

That the mothers' sons are gone because they indoctrinated them with garbage ideologies. That someone should push AK-47s into their guts and pistols against their teeth. That what they need is to be roughed up, shut up. That what goes around comes around.

December 11

Through extended study of my recorded interviews, I note certain trends that emerge over time, illustrating the character of local consensus on the topic to be consistent with Zara's observations.

Sofia: My son came home and told me that he found work.

Lira: A man had come to town looking for laborers for a nearby construction project, and my son was hired.

Mimi: He would be gone several months.

Juliet: That he would send home as much as he could, as soon as he could.

Arlene: I hated that he would be gone for so long, but my son has always been a hard worker, and he knew we needed the help.

Gloria: I thought it was strange, more likely that he had misunderstood the offer, because my boy had never worked before.

It's a persistent enough pattern that it would allow one to form a clear theory, if one were so inclined.

December 15

It's the kind of hypothetical scenario that doesn't get spoken aloud at all, and then only in confidence in closed rooms, but then little by little in places where it doesn't matter who's listening, and then finally in places where the greatest number of listeners will be reached.

The mothers are learning how to speak into megaphones. Two by two they approach the center of the crowd outside state and municipal buildings. They take turns. One holds the speaker high above her head; one leans into the perforated metallic mouth of the device and takes a deep breath.

Hypothetical scenario #1,734:

The boys are lured with the promise of temporary work in another town, or rounded up against their will. They're loaded into the back of a truck. They're driven to an undisclosed location. When they get out of the truck, there are soldiers waiting who order them to strip down and dress in the guerrilla fatigues of the insurgents that are handed to them.

No one bothers with blindfolds, so the boys can see each other, although they try not to look around because of the heaviness around their eyes and the slight tremor of their hands as they button and zip their bodies into the borrowed clothes. Some keep a strange poise, peel off their own shirts and jeans with the calm of kids stripping down to swim in the river. One of the boys has a trembling eye that keeps shifting back to the surrounding mountains. They might make out the sound of a nearby river if they could stop listening to their breathing, their hearts pumping in their ears, while they wait for the signal from the one who seems to be in charge, the order that will trigger what comes next.

The rest happens quickly. One of the soldiers yells, *Fire.* Everyone hits the ground.

December 29

When the phone calls started, the mothers understood that although no one inside the state and municipal buildings was formally taking their cases into consideration, their actions were not going unnoticed.

The mothers didn't want to talk to the men who called because they didn't like their voices. They didn't like the content of the calls. But the men wouldn't stop calling. The calls were always the same.

Hello? they asked. Who is it?

To which the callers on the other end replied, Get out of town. Your name is on the list. Or, Your days are numbered. Or, We know where you live and where your daughter goes to school.

The callers spoke like fortune tellers, like clichés. The mothers would hang up the phone, shudder, say, Jesus.

And their daughters said, Mom. Mama? Who was that?

Nobody, baby, they said. Another wrong number.

January 5

Clarice's family has an uncle new to town, but not a mother, I note from the security of a parked car fifty meters from their home, so it makes sense that I haven't come into contact with them. I have been driving by and camping out for stints, habitually, over the course of the last week, observing who enters and who exits, for how long, and with what regularity. I record all figures, dates, and times in my notebook.

Here, I have a different strategy that I don't fully understand, except to say that it does not represent the best interests of my personal safety: sitting in parked cars with a notebook, driving slowly in rented cars with plates from the capital and dimmed headlights, knocking on the locked doors of unfamiliar homes, my recording device already documenting everything from deep inside my pocket, without a clear script of the questions I've come to ask.

Can I help you? a man asks as he opens the door to Clarice's family's house.

I blink and falter for a moment. I have grown accustomed to speaking only with women and girls.

Can I help you? the man says again.

I want—, I begin, though my lip quivers. I want to know about the boys.

The man laughs. He lifts the bottom flap of his shirt to show the waistband of his jeans, where I see the glimmer of silver on each side.

Ask away, old man, he says, his eyes hard on mine.

I retreat slowly, taking a few steps backward, my right foot catching on a rock and sending me off balance.

No more questions? He advances, but I am already running toward the car. I fumble with the key in the ignition. He lets me start the car, and only once I pull away does he begin to shoot into the spaces in the dirt around my tires.

January 8

For two months Zara will ride her bike all over town. She will feel powerful, a free agent, stronger than a boy. She runs errands for her mother, races cars, breezes past all the other uniformed girls walking toward the school without bearing witness to even a half phrase of gossip.

It's at such moments, with the wind in her face and the blood pumping like crazy through her legs, that she feels closest to her brother.

By the time she's surrounded on the outskirts of town by four men with machetes and told to dismount the bike, she will have gotten very good at starting and stopping, braking on a dime, making left turns in traffic, pedaling uphill, coasting. Zara will look from the edges of the blades in their hands to her handlebars and back again. She will have only a few seconds to consider her options, an expression that is misleading in that it gives the illusion of choice within a context in which all possible actions lead to the same end.

February 17

Writing this from the balcony of my living tower, I have no way of knowing whether the first part of what I've written is true. I never saw Zara again. I can imagine how the bike made her feel, but what do I know about how anything at all appears to a girl from the seat of her bike?

The rest of her story I have pieced together through spotty communication I've exchanged with the mothers over the course of the last few weeks since I returned to the capital. There's more to any story when there are witnesses willing to testify. The mothers have told me lurid details—sounds that were heard, pieces of clothing that were found. I steer my brain away as fast as possible. Bottom line: Queenie and Zara are both officially missing.

Due to concern for my personal safety, I have all but restricted my movement to my living tower. I am writing this from inside my locked apartment, waiting to get on a flight home, any day now, just as soon as my consulate advises me of the most prudent course of action.

A.

When I apply for the small government travel grant that would give me the funding to translate Petritus's book, R.'s mother tells me that she will be on sabbatical for the semester anyway, and she won't need the extra help for the several months that I will be gone.

Besides, she says to me in confidence, you should be looking for another job. I mean, don't get me wrong, R. will be sorry to see you go, but this is just a stopgap for you.

What do you mean? I ask.

I guess I mean that you have a few advanced degrees, R.'s mother says.

I shrug slightly. Yes, I say, but in the humanities.

Anyway, think about what you might actually like to do with your life, R.'s mother says. It is helpful to have women like R.'s mother and mine around to remind me that I have such benefits at my disposal. Without them, it is easy to feel disoriented by the immediate and pressing necessities of rent and feeding myself on a weekly basis.

I never have a chance to tell N. that I've begun translating the book. It is several weeks after we stopped speaking that I decide to apply for the funding. After I find out that I've won the grant, I want to call him to tell him. But every time I pick up the phone, my throat feels tight. I board a flight to his birthplace without saying a word about it; it will be a relief to be across an international border where a call to him would be more complicated to complete and require greater foresight. I keep telling myself, N. didn't hurt me, not really. Still, I feel betrayed by his desire, his force. Even as I leave, and rupture the reign of the present, I realize that I don't want him to know. I want to keep imagining him going to all the regular spots on the rotation of nights we had both memorized, dancing for hours while wondering how many more songs would pass before he would run into me.

In the airplane, I am seated beside a businessman who likes to talk. I don't like to talk, but this few-hour alliance takes my mind off the anxiety of landing, the first few hours in a foreign place: strange-colored currency spitting out of the ATM, the negotiation with the first taxi driver, finding my way to the room in a shared apartment I have rented.

I'm first generation, the businessman says. So when I come back, I feel like I'm home and like I'm away at once. It's like longing for something even while you're inside the thing.

How often do you come back? I ask him.

At least twice per fiscal year, he says.

He asks me why I'm on the plane.

I tell him about the grant and Petritus's book. The fact that I have received a small grant to translate it serves as a helpful anecdote to explain what I'm doing here, even if I'm not sure that I'll actually do anything with the translation when I finish it.

He says, Wow, are you going to try to turn it into a movie?

A movie? I ask.

I mean, it sounds like great material for Hollywood.

I stretch out the corners of my mouth politely as I pull down my tray for coffee.

* * *

When we touch down in the mountainous capital where Tomas Petritus drafted *Field Notes*, I am immediately sickened by the altitude. I push my head back into the headrest and close my eyes.

Hey, says the businessman. Are you okay?

I feel dizzy, I tell him. I feel nauseous.

How are you getting to your hotel? he asks. Do you want to split a taxi?

I'm staying with friends near Park Lourdes, I say. The friends are people I have never met, contacted through an acquaintance of one of my former students, who have rented a room at a marked-up rate to a foreigner who can afford to pay it. But I don't say this to the businessman.

Okay, he says. My hotel is on your way, so let's ride together.

I am relieved at his practical chivalry. Thank god, I think, for businessmen.

But the taxi ride throws a dash of motion sickness into my altitude problem. I watch the bends in each successive mountain we climb and watch the lights in them glimmer in the distance. Night is falling over the capital. As we get closer, I start to double over in my seat.

When we pull up to the businessman's hotel, the doors are opened for us by white-gloved bellboys. They unload the businessman's suitcases and my camping backpack together onto a cart, as if we are traveling together. My backpack looks incongruous beside his matching luggage on the rolling cart, as I gaze forward at it trying to find an object in the distance to train my focus on, to stop everything from spinning.

Hey, I'm worried about you, says the businessman.

I'll be okay, I say.

Do you have a friend you can call? he says.

I have come with two contacts, two people who know of my project and my presence in a country where I otherwise don't know a soul: Henry Paura was Petritus's editor at Semicolon Press; Edgar List is an archive librarian at the Public Library of the People. Prior to boarding, I ran my fingers over their full names, institutions, and contact information as they appear in my phone, and this gave me a sense of calm, purpose, direction.

But I do not call them now.

I'm just going to sit on a bench for a while.

The businessman goes to check in, and says, Wait for me here.

The bellboys push my backpack into the businessman's hotel, along with his luggage set, and I gasp to intervene, but the bell-boys have already rolled everything into the lobby.

As I am crouched over on the bench, I see the hotel staff's eyes linger in my direction. I don't make sense here. My skin is light enough and my hair is thin enough that they seem to think I should be allowed to sit on the bench in front of a space like this, but still, something is not adding up here, their eyes seem to say.

Five minutes later the businessman returns. He says, They carried your bag up with mine. Why don't you come up and rest for a few minutes before you go to Park Lourdes?

I decide I will not go up to a strange man's hotel room in a foreign country to rest for a while. But when I open my eyes my stomach drops again, and I begin to feel a tightness in the back of my throat like I'm going to be sick on the sidewalk in front of the businessman's fancy hotel lobby. I give him my hand, and he escorts me into the elevator.

The businessman's room is on the twentieth floor. He leads me to the king-size bed and helps me lie down.

I'm going to take a shower, he says. Why don't you close your eyes for a few minutes?

I close my eyes, and immediately I begin to dream. I am inside of an operating room, and I am surrounded by doctors and nurses, preparing needles for my arm, stirrups for my ankles. Sensors are stuck one by one onto my chest. As one of the nurses opens the folds of my hospital gown, she says, What a beautiful suntan you have. Such pretty olive skin.

Thank you, I say to the nurses, trying to hide how afraid I am.

As the doctor introduces the needle into my arm, the nurses rub the insides of my thighs with their gloved fingers to relax me on the table.

There, there, they say.

I wake up to someone shaking me after the surgery, but it's not the nurses I expect. It's the businessman. I sit up with a start.

Are you feeling better? he says. You've been asleep for forty-five minutes.

I stand quickly, and immediately the view knocks me out. It is now full night, and the twinkling lights in the distance are ablaze in the mountains, and when I squint my eyes, they all flatline and combine, make new shapes.

I'm sorry, I say. I'm feeling much better. I should go.

Whenever you're ready, I'll walk you downstairs to get a taxi, he says. No rush.

I am in awe of this businessman with his fine white linens and his matching luggage and his luxurious view of the capital and his impeccable manners. As I gather my backpack onto my two shoulders and wait for the elevator, I catch myself thinking of how proud I am of the businessman for not trying to rape me while I was asleep, and I feel like thanks to this fact I have new energy to descend to the ground floor, and talk to another taxi driver, and install myself in the capital.

I hug the businessman goodbye. He takes down my number into his phone.

I'm here for two weeks, he says. We should get dinner one night.

Sure, I say. Absolutely.

The businessman pays my taxi driver, and I'm on my way.

As we climb higher into the mountains, the driver asks me if this is a business or a residence that we're going to.

A residence, I say.

We pass a square full of young people drinking beers around a paint-splattered statue, then the landscape changes again. There are tents under the expressway. Women in bras and jeans walk slowly beside passing cars in the street.

When we pull up to the apartment I've rented, there are military vehicles blockading the street. The driver says something to them, but I don't catch it.

I meet my roommates at 10 p.m. They have been waiting up for me, and they seem irritated.

Petritus came to this country as an outsider to write in a foreign language. That's one part of what drew me to him. The other part is N., because he's the one who got me reading this story. But N. is dead to me, I remind myself. That's what I keep saying to myself as if it were a mantra, because if I don't, I see him everywhere—on the bus, in line to buy bread, in colloquial expressions spoken on the radio, in the laugh of the boy who gives me directions, in the posture of half the men in town.

Regardless, there are dozens of daily reminders of the city from which I came, a place whose name is printed on a quarter of all the T-shirts and ball caps worn here—an image toward which this place is always looking, leaning, even if sometimes only to spit over its shoulder in that general direction. Everyone has a cousin there. Everyone has an uncle, a brother, a friend, a lover; a story that starts or ends there.

I walk toward the Public Library of the People.

But when I arrive, I decide to pass by its heavy iron gates and brick facade and continue walking. I walk until I get lost in warehouse-sized farmers' markets where the fruits and vegetables are stacked—exaggerated and enormous, like produce on steroids—teetering dangerously on the edges of shelves. At your service, the farmers say, brandishing their pocketknives, ready to slice off a sliver of anything I may want to sample. They give preemptive slashes to a few fruit skins, showing off brilliant, unexpected insides: pulps and seeds.

I walk into a neighborhood where women line doorways in bras and jeans, painted mouths smiling. At your service, everyone says.

I walk the neighborhoods of the pet supplies, of the auto parts, of the furniture, of the theaters, of the fabrics. Everyone greets me with the same phrase, and I imagine a full life here that would require the gathering of such services, street by street, from so many.

But I'm here only in passing. For the next four months, I have paid for a rented room at the base of a hill in an apartment I share with a couple who have an extra bedroom. They are renting the room exclusively for the extra income. They are not interested in or curious about me at all.

At night the two of them sit in the living room with all the lights out. He selects songs to play, one by one, from his phone that is connected to the speaker and, one by one, she sings the lyrics to him, along with the recorded voices. They are all the same songs that are playing in clubs and bars all over the city, the music that people dance to. But here, there is no dancing, no speaking. A silent pact in the dark of a quiet house.

If I walk in the door and say hi, they look up for a second, like I'm a passing car that has temporarily distracted them, and she just keeps singing.

The first night in the taxi, I was alarmed to find my street closed off to traffic with roadblocks and guarded by armed soldiers.

When I mentioned the roadblock to the couple whose apartment I inhabit, they only shook their heads. Those aren't soldiers, he said, they're the armed brigade. They close the street every night after dark. That's why it's so safe around here.

I nodded, as if this distinction were familiar.

When I ask them for tips on getting to the Public Library of the People or the Museum of Local Living Memory, they only smile and say that they never go to those institutions, that they're only built to generate tourism, not for the people who live here.

It's close to seven now, and I am still in the neighborhood of the fabrics. The sun starts to fall fast, the trick of so many peaks and valleys. The lights begin to switch on in the distance. I squint my eyes toward the mountains until all the unique points of light blur.

Taxis slow for me, honking to see if I need a ride. But I wave them ahead; I prefer to walk, I tell myself, while my mind can't help itself from reproducing the concrete details of every story I've ever been told that involves two surprise extra passengers at the next stoplight, a handgun, a blindfold, and every ATM in town.

An older woman packing up her juice stand for the night leans in my direction when I linger at the intersection where she works.

Clarion and Ninety-Eighth? I ask her.

Here, when I get lost, I talk to people to ask for directions. There are certain conditions that make it easier to express vulnerability in a language that's not my own. When people notice my accent, they're polite enough to only wrinkle the corners of their mouths and keep talking.

Straight ahead, she says, pointing to the left of the direction I was walking in. You're not so far.

She points to my purse, slung lazily around my shoulder. I start to dig around in search of spare coins, before I feel her reach and shift the weight of my purse so it rests directly in front of my body. She grabs my hand and places it firmly across the broken zipper.

Walk like this, she says. Understand?

I nod. I walk straight ahead like she tells me to until I see the armed brigade and roadblocks that let me know I've made it home.

I live here, I say, approaching the soldier closest to me. The echo of my heavy consonant sounds lingers in the air between us. The soldier cocks his head and nearly smiles as he lowers his rifle. I watch him take in the sight of me: sunglasses propped on top of my head like a second set of eyes, right hand still grasping hard at the flaps of my purse as if it contained a wild animal I cannot let loose. I live here, I insist, and though we both know that this statement is only one part true, tonight, as every other night, they wave me in.

The morning I decide to call Edgar List at the Public Library of the People, he greets me generously, tells me to come by right away. He is an elderly gentleman with meticulously pressed shirts and old-fashioned handwriting who says he would be very happy to help facilitate my research. When I learned that the original manuscript pages of *Field Notes* were housed within the archive he oversees, I wrote to him, describing my project and requesting he serve as an in-country contact for my grant application. He agreed immediately and sent a formal letter of support typed on the letterhead of the Public Library of the People. When I received the letter, I felt immediately ashamed for his blind faith in me, as if I had somehow deceived him regarding the extent of my credentials. Now, I write my requests for archival materials on little slips of pink paper, and Edgar disappears into the back with them. When he returns with plastic-wrapped stacks of papers, he winks at me as he passes them across the counter.

Thank you, I say.

Anytime, my dear, says Edgar, I'm here until eight.

I sit at one of the long study tables in the library, crossing and uncrossing my legs, adjusting my cloth gloves, palming through documents.

The original pages of *Field Notes* housed in the archives include material that was cut from the book, complete with handwritten marginalia and commentary. All of Petritus's most trusted editors and readers seem to have been here in the capital. Although the manuscript was entrusted to the library by an anonymous donor, the fact that it was heavily edited by the local poet Rita Zapo, with whom Petritus shared an editor, suggests she may have had a hand in its preservation and posthumous publication. Rita Zapo is documented as a longtime friend and confidant to Petritus. She was the first female winner of the prestigious Echo poetry prize, but she was killed before she had a chance to follow up on her debut collection.

I open the manuscript and find Petritus's typed pages and biographical information. As always, the author is a nonentity, consistent only in his steady erasure of significant details about himself. Editorial feedback from outside readers was systematically accepted or rejected by Petritus with his system of marking a plus or a minus sign beside each critique to signify whether he would consider the suggestion. In the manuscript version, Zapo's cursive hand, wildly scribbled in every margin, contrasts with the order of his neat symbols. And yet, Petritus was clearly comfortable with Zapo's criticism, judging by the quantity of plus signs beneath her comments. She often chided him for his awkward constructions or cultural assumptions. In the margins of the pages in my hand, Zapo comes off as somewhere between pedantic and enraged. Her handwriting circles and strikes through passages, offers criticism in her scrawled cursive.

I am mentally constructing frail lifelines, thick as telephone wires, between every visible window on the block, Petritus writes.

In the margin Zapo scrawls, *Lazy metaphor. Literal fat telephone wires everywhere.*

+, responds Petritus.

The cat plays with a moth the size of a bird while I work, and I pretend I'm too busy to intervene while I watch her chew off one of its wings, reads another line in Petritus's manuscript.

Meanwhile half of the town is in body bags. Who cares! writes Zapo below.

+, concludes Petritus in agreement.

On another page, Zapo has scratched out an entire section, attributed to one of the mothers in Petritus's manuscript, so the page has been transformed into an elaborate structure of scribbles, with only the repetition of the lower bellies of vowels left visible. I can still make out the words just enough to read it, and from its placement in the larger draft, I can imagine which mother is cited as speaking these words only because of the shock of curls and graceful limp that is attributed to her a few lines before:

I lost my land.
I lost my right leg.
Above the knee.
And I lost my home.

The annotated discussion that follows in a series of scratched-out plus and minus signs suggests that Zapo and Petritus disagreed about the use of this passage. According to other sources, in the weeks following an early serialized run of this excerpt from the manuscript, Zapo became convinced that the lines of the passage were taken verbatim from one of the mothers on whom Petritus based his research, and from whom he did not obtain written consent.

In the years following Petritus's return to his homeland, Zapo was reported to have been sighted in the capital's bookstores, lingering over copies of the journal that published this excerpt, pretending to browse, and—when the cashiers' backs were turned—ripping the page out. She denied all accusations of having ever done this.

It's a binding error, the responsibility of the publisher, she argued in print on multiple occasions when questioned about the missing page, even in instances when the page shows a clear tear.

Unsurprisingly, there is no official record of Petritus's thoughts on the passage, but one can only assume that he eventually came around to Zapo's criticism because the final published book does not include it.

Even though I am in another country, I involuntarily keep a mental schedule of the rotation of live music taking place each night in the city. I try to fill my evenings with other commitments—films, tours—but they are naturally sparse in a place where I know no one, and so it's unsurprising that every Monday I imagine the vast expanse of the wooden floors at Telex; that on Wednesdays my brain conjures up the sticky booths at Mina's where we lace up our shoes or drink beer; that on Thursdays I always remember the old woman who works the door to the basement at Ciel, who collects our covers brandishing a stamp for our wrists in her shaky hand. It is inevitable on all these nights, but especially on Fridays, when the city's dancers descend upon the pier, that I conjure up N.'s neck and waist as he completes a turn, his hand clamped softly around the fingers of some woman, and imagine I were in her place.

I run over conversations from the last night we saw each other again and again in my mind, trying to uncover a new wrinkle, a new pattern or narrative thread.

Why are you playing with me? he asked me.

I'm not, I said.

You've been sleeping in my bed with me for eight months. Why don't you sleep in your own bed?

I looked at the ceiling, briefly.

I don't sleep well there, I said finally.

You don't sleep well here either, he said.

I like you, I said. I'd rather sleep next to you.

That's what I mean, skinny, he said. Why do you like playing with me like this?

I remember staring up at the ceiling again, but I must have been dreaming because when I woke up to N.'s body on top of mine, I was frightened.

I gasped, but I didn't take my eyes off his.

He was stronger than me, I knew that I couldn't move, so I didn't try. Later, I thought, I could have yelled to wake up the couple who slept in the living room. But in the moment, I didn't feel that was an option.

Like N. had said, Why was I there anyway? Why wasn't I in my own bed across town? Why would I interrupt the sleep of people who had to be up for work in a few hours?

When I dial the number that the businessman has given me, I don't know exactly why I'm calling. It feels at once rude not to call and rude to call. We meet for dinner in a restaurant near his hotel. I understand without asking that the businessman will feel uncomfortable in the leafy neighborhoods around Park Lourdes where I am staying. His family has told him that these neighborhoods are dangerous.

When over dinner he asks me what I've been up to, I mention some of the places—museums, parks, boulevards—where I have been spending time.

Be careful, he says to me. It's important for a woman, and a foreign woman especially, to be careful here.

I look at a piece of sky just over the businessman's head. I am always careful, I say, wondering what world he imagines I live in that he thinks I need to be told. That a well-meaning and kind man like the businessman is stupid enough to think I haven't internalized living in a woman's body enough to view all external stimuli as potential threats.

After dinner, he takes me dancing. His leads are heavy. He squeezes my hands and never releases them long enough for me to spin out and feel my steps unencumbered by his design.

When later he asks me where I learned to dance, I tell him about how I used to go out every night in the city. And when he asks me why, I say how I am attracted to the conversation, the communication—in the instant. He frowns.

I don't see it that way at all, he says. I see it as a form of expression.

But there are two people expressing themselves, I say. That's a conversation.

But there is one leader, he says.

I smile and pretend not to care.

When he asks me at the end of the night if I'd like to come back to his hotel with him, I answer honestly.

I'm actually really very tired, I say.

There's a lot of static on the line when I call Henry Paura at Semi-colon Press, and at first I'm not sure if I'll get through at all. His voice breaks, solid but strained, like I've woken him up from a nap.

What can I do for you? he asks.

I explain who I am, remind him I'm translating one of his authors, tell him I have some questions about Petritus and his post-humous book.

Henry suggests we meet in a fashionable district with many international restaurants that will accommodate any dietary restrictions I may have.

I don't have any dietary restrictions, I try to say, but Henry has already selected a place. We make a date for lunch. I write it in my planner, even though I'm unlikely to forget because it is the only thing that I have penciled in all week.

When I walk up to the restaurant at the scheduled hour, Henry is already seated, wearing dark glasses and a black scarf despite the sun. He waves me to his table, looking annoyed. A man with a pickup truck full of lemons is driving in slow circles around the block, saying into a microphone, *Lemons, get your lemons, five for one, ten for two.*

I went ahead and ordered a carafe of coffee, Henry says.

Great, I say, overcompensating with a smile.

How are you finding the city? asks Henry. How is your project going?

Well, I think. But I have some questions.

Of course you do, Henry says. Let's see if I can't help clear up some of your confusion.

I stutter for a moment, then clear my throat. I say, I guess I hoped some of my research here in the capital would help me learn more about the author of *Field Notes*. But everywhere I look for Tomas Petritus, I come up with nothing. He's a dead end. There's more information in the archives about editorial feedback the manuscript received from his readers than there is on Petritus himself. I'm starting to wonder if he ever existed outside of this book.

Henry blinks, pulls out a cigarette, holds up the soft pack to me to offer one before lighting it. He says, That's the thing, isn't it.

The thing? I repeat.

The man in the pickup truck passes again. *Lemons, get your lemons, five for one, ten for two, Lemons, get your lemons, five for one, ten for two.* He says it so many times that the words stop being words and start to shift into nonsensical sounds.

Henry inhales, breathes out. Would it change anything if he didn't exist? he asks.

I'm translating him, I say.

Henry shrugs like this doesn't count.

You're his editor, I say. You tell me.

Henry looks briefly up to the sky, as if for guidance, before meeting my eyes again.

Rita Zapo wrote *Field Notes*, he says.

As soon as Henry says this aloud, I understand that in some unconscious part of my brain this suspicion had already started to grow.

But it's published with Petritus's name, I insist.

Henry smiles. Do you think anyone here would have paid attention to a book of testimonial prose from a female poet? Do you think any readers in your language will care about its translation? How many copies will you sell of the posthumous book, five hundred at best? A thousand if you're very lucky?

I tighten my lips into a neutral half smile because the truth is that the thought has never crossed my mind.

Let me assure you that it's all pretty irrelevant, Henry says. And no great secret. Anyone who digs long enough will come to the same conclusion you're on your way to making. I'm saving you some time. Consider it a favor.

And you knew that before you published it?

Henry nods. Naturally it was Rita's decision; it had nothing to do with me, he says. Rita thought someone like Petritus would generate different kinds of readers, you understand.

I shake my head.

A prose writer. A foreign, male prose writer, Henry continues. But you'll notice—if you were familiar with her work at all, I mean, you'd notice—that she gave little effort to disguising her own voice, or to inventing a realistic biography for Petritus. She had been receiving threats of course as well, so she likely viewed it as a safety measure. Ultimately, it didn't matter of course.

I pause, a beat too long, betraying my ignorance.

Because of what happened to Zara? I ask.

No, says Henry, without masking his annoyance.

I nod, I look down at the ashtray between us and wait for him to continue.

Because of what happened to Rita, says Henry finally.

I nod, mumbling something about a reference to Rita Zapo's death in the archives that I didn't investigate because I didn't see it as relevant to my project at the time.

Henry looks at me hard, stubbing out his cigarette, and raises his hand to signal the waiter.

I return to the Public Library of the People and sit down at a table with new search terms.

All the first materials to surface are newspaper stories, dated fifteen years ago, with titles like "Celebrated Female Poet's Murder Raises Questions About Ties to Guerrilla Organization," and "Mothers United Representative Condemns Female Poet's Death as Act of State-Sponsored Terror." I take the elevator to the third-floor archives and Edgar fulfills my request for relevant photos and newspaper clippings related to Rita Zapo.

Captioned photographs published in the local newspapers include:

A heavily made-up Zapo drinking from a juice box at the corner of Beach Road and Thirty-Seventh Street.

Zapo in a floral-print dress, standing at a microphone alongside a panel of men in front of the National Library.

Zapo giving a speech at a podium, receiving the Echo poetry prize.

Zapo lying under a sheet on the sidewalk.

*   *   *

In this final photo of Rita Zapo, her high-heeled shoes stick out from the white sheet that covers her body. I stare at the smooth muscles of her calves in this photo. Despite the sheet obscuring the rest of her, they look like the calves of someone who could get up and dance to whatever song plays next. The crowd that surrounds Zapo is almost exclusively composed of women. This is easily explained, the accompanying article suggests, since Zapo was said to have exited the local branch offices of Mothers United at 7 p.m., when the individual thought to be her assassin was first spotted at the intersection of Saint Rex and Twenty-Third on the back of a motorcycle. As the first shots were fired, the mothers filed out of their offices with the likely intent to intervene.

The article continues, It is common knowledge that the matriarchs of Mothers United are unarmed and unafraid. They are experts in the art of making their bodies visible, by covering themselves in high-gloss, blown-up photographs of missing children, and singing loud out-of-tune songs of hope with undertones of fury in high-traffic urban settings. They are said to be difficult to intimidate. They have been known to use their bodies as human shields.

In the photograph, the mothers surround Zapo's body. There are maybe ten of them in frame. They do not wail, and they do not cover their faces in their hands. For the most part, they assume one of two poses: Either they look dead into the eye of the camera, or they look dead into the eyes of one of the portraits hanging from the sandwich-board-sized photos shrouding their bodies. Only one mother crouches at the side of the poet. In the photograph she seems to be removing a backpack from Zapo's supine body, as if to help her rest.

I start to sense strange things in my gut. I don't know how else to explain it. I feel a fluttering where I imagine my ovaries once were. I know that phantom limb sensations are possible, but I've never heard of this. I perceive the floor of my pelvis drop, a rankling around in my insides. I want to go to the doctor, but I wait, because I don't know where to go; because it's probably nothing; because I no longer have reproductive organs; because my vocabulary for reproductive terminology in this language is not so strong.

But while I don't go, an ache starts to take root in me.

It grows as this feeling grows.

I walk to the Museum of Local Living Memory, where—among catalogs of other recent atrocities—there are thoughtfully curated timelines that chart key statistical information and personal details regarding the assassinations of journalists, writers, photographers, students, union leaders, community organizers, and prospective political candidates. Rita Zapo is among them. Often, though not always, references to military and financial intervention from my own country obscure questions of culpability for these murders.

There is a set of headphones that hangs from a peg on the wall beneath the same iconic photos: Zapo receiving the Echo prize at the National Library, Zapo's body covered with a sheet surrounded by mothers. When I take the headphones off the wall and place them over my ears, I hear Zapo's final recorded interview prior to her death:

INTERVIEWER: It's been five years since you published your last collection, for which you were awarded the Echo prize. What's next for you as a poet?

ZAPO: I'm not writing any poetry at the moment.

INTERVIEWER: Should I interpret that to mean you're exploring new genres?

ZAPO: [coughs] Sure, that sounds good.

INTERVIEWER: Your editor, Henry Paura, has suggested that you have been writing prose. Any truth to that?

ZAPO: I find it amusing that Henry would conclude that based on something I mentioned to him in passing of which he hasn't read a single word.

INTERVIEWER: So then, for the record, you're not writing at all.

ZAPO: I'm writing regular essays for the *Weekly Independent*. Maybe you've seen them?

INTERVIEWER: [long pause] Some critics have dismissed your recent journalism as political propaganda.

ZAPO: [mumbles something unintelligible]

INTERVIEWER: How would you describe your involvement in the underground network Mothers United, where your presence has been noted at regular demonstrations?

ZAPO: I hold up their umbrellas and megaphones while they speak, and I listen to their stories.

INTERVIEWER: What would your response be to those who allege that the mothers are accessories to a terrorist organization?

ZAPO: I would ask them to go do fifteen seconds of research on the topic before the next time they decide to open their mouths.

INTERVIEWER: It's been a pleasure speaking with you, Ms. Zapo.

ZAPO: The pleasure is all mine.

In the obituary excerpt displayed beside the photograph, Rita Zapo is credited for her prize-winning poetry collection and her regular journalism in the last year of her life chronicling the work of Mothers United, whose demonstrations continue to be held each Tuesday afternoon in the capital. There is no mention of *Field Notes* anywhere.

When I arrive at the demonstration, it looks like the mothers have already been out there for a while. I can't help myself from feeling like the peripheral narrator of the notes I've spent the last six months inside of as I find a spot to stand just outside the border of their circle.

The mothers carry umbrellas of all different colors as an antidote to the afternoon sun. They fan themselves as well, sometimes with the newspaper, sometimes with collapsible plastic fans that they produce from the insides of their purses. Some of them have little spray bottles with water inside that they mist onto each other's necks and faces.

They all wear white blouses. They all carry a colorful plastic flower in one hand. They take turns with the megaphone, but there is one mother who serves as a kind of emcee: introducing new speakers, singing the first verses of the songs before the other mothers join in. Some of their stories, I notice, I know already, as soon as they start speaking. I'm not sure if it's because Rita Zapo took them all down verbatim, but it doesn't take long to anticipate the end of any story from its beginning. Between each speaker, they slowly repeat these words over and over again: Mothers United is not and will never be part of the violence. The work of Mothers United is always to seek the truth.

When one of the mothers sees me standing off to the side of the demonstration, she offers me a plastic flower to hold and a sheet of paper, which is a photocopy of the lyrics to the songs they sing. I thank her. I remain for a full two hours. I watch her from across the square, but she never speaks into the microphone. She wears a white blouse with large details of butterflies. When I look for her to return the plastic flower and photocopied song sheet at the end of the demonstration, she's gone.

I come home from the demonstration, and I try to make a call to N. The line rings and rings, but I don't know if it's because I have the international prefixes mixed up or because N. isn't there.

I want to tell him I'm here. I want to ask him about Rita Zapo and the mothers, to ask him what he knew, what his mother knew. There are so many things I want to tell N.; he is often the first person I want to call any time something happens. But then I remember how he looked at me the last time, as I boarded the train, how he never tried to contact me again, not even to apologize or explain. I remind myself: N. is dead to me, or I am dead to him. I wish I could remember more clearly what words were exchanged between us that provoked this conclusion. I feel guilty for stealing the book, and I feel angry for feeling guilty. Then, I become unsure whether I want to speak to him, what it was we were to each other. So I hang up the line before I can decide, before I grow tired of waiting, before he has a chance to answer.

The more I play the scene over in my head, the more unsure I become. Questions like these rise and fall through my mind:

Did N. really want to hurt me, or does my memory exaggerate the experience?

Had he pushed my hands into the bed before or after I woke up?

Could I really not move my hands under his?

Had we been speaking in my language or in his?

The rankling through my insides continues. I touch my belly, and I imagine that there has been some mistake, that my body was never opened up and emptied of the possibility of carrying a child. As I trace my fingers along the crest of my scar, I know that this is impossible, but the more the feeling keeps me up at night, the more I wish this were true.

I decide that when morning comes, I will write to the city hospital where my medical history is housed and request that my full file be sent to me.

I walk to the site of the demonstration, and I learn that the mothers have offices in the center of town. I walk to the building. A man greets me at the first floor.

Who are you here to see? he asks.

Mothers United? I say.

Oh, too bad, you just missed them. They left for lunch. Come back in an hour.

As I exit the building where their offices are housed, I pause. The bakery marquee at the intersection where Rita Zapo's last photo was taken, before her body was carried away under a sheet, still glows in the same spot fifteen years later. It's then that I notice a small stone laid into the cement of the sidewalk, with granite lettering etched into it.

THIS IS THE SITE OF THE MURDER OF THE LOCAL FEMALE POET RITA ZAPO. MAY SHE REST IN PEACE.

Beside it, someone has written in black spray paint, *Terrorist bitch*. And someone else has crossed that out and scrawled below, *Pray for us sinners*.

When I return to the offices of the mothers, the doorman sends me up. Unit 5, up five flights of stairs.

Hello, I call into the barred entrance. Good afternoon?

Good afternoon, dear, I hear someone say. I hear the squeak of a chair pushed on the tile floor, and a small woman with faint purple hair slowly enters my vision.

I'm looking for the office of Mothers United, I say.

Then you've come to the right place, says the woman, slowly working her fingers through the combination lock that holds the gate between us shut.

What can I do for you? the woman asks.

I was at your demonstration the other day. I'm a translator, I say. For Rita Zapo.

The woman clucks her tongue and crosses herself quickly as she pulls open the metal gate. She takes my hands in hers, and I crouch to greet her. I feel like a giant, nearly twice her size.

I'm Jasmin, the director, she says. How kind of you to come.

She asks me how I take my tea.

As we turn the corner to the back office, I start to hear a growing roar of voices. There are thirty to forty women seated around a table, drinking tea and cross-stitching. Jasmin escorts me into the back of the room. Today, she says, the mothers are participating in a workshop to cross-stitch tapestries for next week's action. They are going to drape every tree in the square outside the mayor's office with a tapestry that says: REPENT, COWARDS. They are working on other cross-stitched tapestries that will say: THE VOICE OF THE PEOPLE WILL NOT BE SILENCED, and: HEY MOMS, STAY VIGILANT!

Jasmin says, The women here have suffered greatly. They are all migrants from other places. Not a single one is from the capital. They were mostly field laborers. They have had to start again here. Rita was a beautiful collaborator, god rest her soul. She performed interviews with the mothers, and she published essays decrying the massacres before anyone else wanted to touch our stories.

But what about her book *Field Notes*? I'm translating it.

Jasmin shakes her head slowly. There you are confused, dear. Rita had been a poet. But she swore off writing anything but journalism for years.

Several days later I arrive home at night to find a package waiting for me. I tear away at the heavy cardboard envelope, and I find a manila envelope inside. There are roughly a hundred pages bound together by a large rubber band. The first sheet is blank, and as I slip off the rubber band to free the others, I imagine they are photocopies of additional parts of the manuscript that have been sent by Henry from Semicolon, or by Edgar from the library.

There is a note on top of the pile with the following message scrawled in black marker:

Per your request.

The next thing I notice is an anatomical sketch of a woman's reproductive system, and several smaller sketches beside it. The labeled sketches seem familiar to me. My first instinct is that the reason for this is that everything is written in my native language. I flip quickly through the pages and take in my full name, date of birth, and account identification number, printed inside the official seal of the city on every top right corner.

The folder contains the detailed copy of my own medical records I had requested, and with it the unequivocal documentation that a child will never grow inside of me.

I think back to how after the surgery, my case was transferred from the care of the oncologist to that of a specialized gynecologist. She spoke to me alone in her office, without the entourage of rotating residents.

It's a shame, she said, that there isn't more documented research to rely on. We've been preemptively pulling out organs as a caution when this kind of cell growth shows up; that's how it's always been done. But women's bodies are understudied, even now.

I am certain that I am not the only one who was hurt by the fact that women's bodies are understudied, that other women exist who have fallen hard on the same truth. But I don't know these women; I don't know their names, I don't know their stories. I don't belong to Queenie and Lexus and Sofia, but I take comfort in their sense of community. In my private and unexpressed pain, I recognize that it's something I don't share.

I stroke my gutted belly. I close my eyes.

Later that night, as I lie in bed, I think, again, about being pinned under N.'s body, and it occurs to me what it is that hurts. N. broke the spell between us, unspoken as it was sacred, which now feels muddied, like it was never anything at all. Like I was only ever a warm body to him. Like he was only ever a warm body to me.

My heart cramps to remember how we only told each other half the truth of our stories, how we consumed one another's affection and curiosity and patience and warmth and body heat and half-truths over the course of many months.

I don't forgive him, but I also don't know how much longer I expected the spell could last before shifting, inevitably, into something else.

I heard you talking to our director about Rita, someone says.

I turn around and see a mother I never noticed. She approaches me slowly, a cane in her left hand.

I was there the day she died, she says. I knew her. The woman nods. Diane, says the woman, extending her hand, which I take into mine.

I'm translating *Field Notes*, I say.

It was published under a pseudonym, so it's rarely attributed to her, Diane says.

She watches this bit of information land in my expression, and she sees it does not surprise me.

What else do you know about Rita? Diane asks me.

That she stopped writing poetry after she won the Echo prize. That she was murdered on this block. I've read her journalism about Mothers United, I say.

Do you know why Rita Zapo stopped writing poetry?

No.

I have some tapes that might interest you, old recordings. If you don't mind coming around the house, I'll share them with you.

I will wish later that I had never agreed, that I never learned the reason why Rita Zapo stopped writing poetry, that I was never invited into Diane's home with the tape recorder and the shoebox full of cassettes.

Her house is in a peripheral neighborhood up the slope of a mountain. I take two trains and a bus from the center and cross the capital. I have to take a taxi the rest of the way. When I arrive at the agreed-upon intersection, Diane is there waiting for me. I follow her around the corner and up the base of a hill. Despite her cane and her age, she walks with grace. My calves are unaccustomed to the terrain, and I need to pace myself. When we reach the house, there is a cake prepared and sweet tea. Diane cuts a piece of cake and pours a cup without my asking. The house is quiet, remains quiet, and I suspect she lives alone. When I ask her if that is the case, she confirms it.

She says, I used to live with my son, but now it's just me.

She pulls out an old cassette player, the kind I remember playing alongside grammar school filmstrips. Beside it is a battered Adidas shoebox filled with unmarked tapes.

What are these? I ask Diane.

Conversations, she says.

I press the PLAY button, and immediately I recognize the dry low voice I heard in the recordings at the Museum of Local Living Memory.

SARAH BRUNI

The tape whirrs in the background. Rita asks, Where do you think your son is?

I listen as Rita asks the question and to the pause that follows. I hear a shallow inhalation, before I hear the same voice begin to respond to the question posed.

I don't know, says the same voice.

I look up from the cassette to Diane, but she only shakes her head, encouraging me to keep listening.

Where is your son? Rita's voice asks again.

I don't fucking know, the same voice—Rita's—responds.

I don't understand, I say.

Diane's fingers flatten against the STOP button and the room goes silent.

So you didn't know? Diane says. I suspected you might not. That's why I wanted you to come and listen for yourself. Rita was a mother too.

Diane explains, Rita showed up at the first demonstration with a flask in her purse and took quick sips at it, as if the speed with which she drank would render this repeated action invisible. She wore earrings made of seeds and shell husks that shook when she walked. Her hands flung in every direction at once when she was excited and sat lifeless in her lap when she was angry. She was tall and very thin. She talked too much.

She attended four protests in total before she had the courage to approach us. She came up to us as we were folding our banners and placing the photos of the boys in a cardboard box.

Where are they, she said. Not a question.

We shook our heads.

Where are the boys? she said again, almost a shout.

We crossed ourselves and said, One day we hope to see them again in the next life, if not in this one.

Fuck the motherfucking next life, Rita said quietly. Why would they leave? Who took them? Are they dead or not?

That's when Jasmin squeezed her hand and invited her to our meeting.

She hiccuped, twice. Then she accepted.

She started writing about us, Diane says. That much is no great secret. Everyone acknowledges her journalism about us. No one talks about the book.

I watch the tremble in Diane's hand as she reaches for the box of tapes that she offers me. She shakes slightly as she stoops after collecting the shoebox and places it in my hand. Her body is determined, forward-pointing, strong.

Rita interviews herself alongside her interviews of the mothers. She speaks into the recording device as if it were a telephone, as if it were a direct line to her missing son: You disappeared several months ago. Seven, eight. I've lost track. But I can report to you that the situation tastes of a long-rotting fruit.

Diane explains, Rita's testimonies sound written because they are. They're all from letters to her son that she wrote; then she read from them into her recording device, when she failed to find an address for him.

I don't understand, I say. Where would she have mailed them?

Her son isn't missing in the same way that ours are, Diana explains. He went to your country, looking for his father.

I'll leave you alone with them, Diane says, as she stands up.

Do you mind if I record them? I ask, holding up my phone.

Whatever you think would be helpful, honey, Diane says.

I hit RECORD on one device and PLAY on the other.

You disappeared several months ago. Seven, eight. I've lost track.
But I can report to you that the situation tastes of a long-rotting
fruit. It is a dull, quiet rot, a taste that is the opposite of hunger or
hope.

    It's very different from the way you showed up, unsolicited.
I felt you multiplying and dividing in some dark part of me,
performing complex mathematical functions beyond our
collective comprehension by intuition alone.

    I was terrified then. I mean, I was exhilarated.

    You were the size of a pumpkin seed, an almond, a berry, a
tangerine before I told anyone.

    I wanted to be completely alone with you.

Before you, I had always been meticulous, careful, fearful of
getting inside of a situation that I could not control. The nuns
at the girls' school of my childhood had instilled in me a sense
of reverence and constant trepidation. They read aloud to us
from the Book of Revelation that laments the position of the
woman with child during the second coming of Christ. She cannot
run, she is anchored to the ground with the weight of another

generation. She's forced to remain in place and withstand all the trials and tribulations. I felt for her, but I also recognized her position as a warning: I would make sure that I'd always be able to run.

A wasp was inside the house today, and I spoke to her with the same voice I used to use to talk to you when you were young.

This wasp was dizzying herself again and again into the closed side of the window, when the other half was wide open. My own shoulder blades ached just witnessing this kind of spectacular futility.

I said to the wasp, Sweetheart, be reasonable.

I tried to coax her outside with soft words and a spoonful of honey poured into the empty lid of a yogurt container. I placed the lid on the windowsill and waited. I left the room. Eventually she did too.

I keep thinking of this while I write to you, even though I hope for the opposite result: that if I open the windows, one day you will be back at the kitchen table.

I have started sleeping with all the doors and windows unlocked, just in case.

I woke up this morning with a memory clear as if you were still here. You were seven years old, a blue crayon gripped tight in your hand, sitting across from me at the kitchen table while I worked.

What are you writing? you asked me.

A poem about a bird.

Am I the bird?

Sure, I said. Why not? I thought.

Then I watched as you began to transform whatever you had been drawing up to that point into a sharp beak and a massive wingspan.

And at the time I hadn't thought anything of it. But now I see you had been right, that I had been writing about you, just not realizing it until you were already gone.

You came to me during school vacation from university. I had been studying poetry and political science, and I didn't yet know it at the time, but we would all return from the campus recess to find our professors were replaced with new ones; the books were exchanged for others too. We would no longer speak of the subject that the classes covered. We would be encouraged to spy on our neighbors. I was nineteen. In the end, you would be my ticket out. I avoided the worst of the worst of those years because of you.

The last day of classes, I walked to the river delta from the Department of Arts and Letters. When I got close to the water, I took off my shoes and pushed my feet into the sand. I hiked up my skirt and waded out to just above my knees. The water was muddy and warm; the waves wet the backs of my thighs but made no sound. I had just begun sharing fragments of writing with my professors, and I had gotten some generous feedback, invitations to participate in a workshop or two the following semester, but I remember thinking, however fleetingly, that none of it mattered. It was odd, because at the time there was nothing that I'd been more invested in than gaining the admiration and encouragement of my mentors, but I sensed then—or anyway, I think now, in retrospect—that things were about to shift.

*During the holidays from classes, I boarded an airplane. I
crossed several mountain ranges and the sea until I landed in the
city that I would later always think of as yours.*

*My mother asked me not to go. I had been floating the idea of the
trip for a while, and she didn't approve. It was dangerous was
her thinking at the time. Still, I wanted to breathe the air there. I
didn't listen. I was like you, headstrong and often daydreaming. It
made me feel so much worse, in the immediate aftermath of the
trip, for having not been careful, for letting them be proven right.
I didn't tell my mother when I left either. I called from a public
telephone when I was already gone. I did call though. And it was
just a two-week trip. I wasn't sure when you first left if you had
the same thing in mind. I was waiting to answer a collect call. For
weeks. I mean, if you still want to call, I will accept the charges. I
know you know that I would answer, but I'm just saying. In case
you ever stop to think, like I did, of your mother at home.*

*I didn't have much of a plan, and that was the point. I got off
the plane and hailed a taxi. The driver was an elderly man who
noticed my limited capacity with the language, and immediately
echoed my mother in telling me to be careful.*

*My first impression was a bevy of markets downtown,
everything you could ever imagine haggling a price for to start
a new life. And I thought about it. I did. Lingerie, light bulbs,
purses, parsnips, parakeets. Everything laid out on blankets
along the street. There were people stumbling around between
the wares; some seemed to belong to the neighborhood, others
looked more lost than I figured I did. I didn't really have the
money for souvenirs, though I thought of buying a small shot
glass with a golden rim and a black pony painted onto the side*

that reminded me of a book I had read as a child. I clutched it in my fist for a few moments just to feel the weight of it and imagine taking a quick gulp from it, before replacing it on its space on the blanket.

I remember I walked to a museum and paid what seemed like a lot of money to enter an exhibition: boxes on pedestals, filled with collages, objects, photographs of birds assembled, mirrors, glasses. I remember a child peering into one of the boxes filled with feathers. The child said something to me that I didn't understand, and I smiled at him anyway—bashfully, but impressed by the general presence of him in the gallery space.

Do you like the birds? I asked him.

His mother took his hand then, and they walked away, even though I was certain I hadn't said anything wrong.

Languages sometimes let you inside them just when you've been underestimated. My face became hot with a mix of shame and anger, hating being judged, even when the assumption was most likely correct. I wonder if you ever found that since you left. Or if you ever became as enraged as I could be.

When I left the gallery, night had fallen over the city, but it was warm enough at night to walk in straw sandals and a cotton dress. It was dark, and I was walking fast, and the sandals were a half size too big. I turned every few blocks or so to make sure I wasn't being followed. But it was still a pleasure to feel the air there, just as I'd imagined. I took in big sips of it the faster I walked.

And that night, walking back to the hotel room, I passed by a bar with filthy windows and filled with music, the giant barreling sound of it pouring out the doors and into the night. I stepped inside, pushed my way to the bar, and ordered a beer. It was the kind of place you could lose yourself and never have to *exchange a word with anyone but feel completely at home with the world.*

Everyone was dancing, but not in neat pairs. The crowd swayed and hopped in rhythm with the music, all together, like one giant breathing organism from another planet. I remember looking up at the tin ceiling in the bar, and at a different tin ceiling in my room before I went to bed, feeling my joints still tingling with electricity, my legs wanting to keep swaying and twitching within the sheets of the narrow hotel bed. I remember giggling myself to sleep, all alone and ecstatic. I felt so alive that night.

You used to ask me about your father, but I only ever told you he was a stranger to us.

I was getting off a train that dead-ended at the sea when the stranger approached me.

He had large brown eyes and curls in his hair that made me want to reach out and trace them with my fingers.

Are you traveling alone? he asked me.

No, I lied. I'm here with my boyfriend. But he's asleep in the hotel.

Let's walk together, he said. I will walk you to a part of the shore that is quiet, far away from your sleeping boyfriend.

He said it like he was joking, but landed heavy on the last word, as if acknowledging the gracelessness of my lie.

But I only grinned. I didn't insist one way or the other. I didn't want to talk too much at first and give myself away as a foreigner. I was grateful to have met someone who knew his way around this part of the outskirts of the city. He was a fast walker, and I made the effort to keep up with his pace. But he started to speak more slowly, picking up, I assumed, on my own unwieldy pace inside his language. It made me feel more bold, this patience, like I could stop worrying so much about vowel sounds and just act a bit more like myself. It was dusk and a little cool. I remember passing my hands into the sleeves of my sweatshirt while we walked.

There was a little tingling at the back of my neck, at my hairline, but I ignored it. I was too determined and uncharacteristically fearless in that moment to do anything except follow, laugh, and—after he pried the cap off a liter of beer he produced from his backpack—take long sips from the bottle.

We walked side by side for a long time. We passed rows of buildings, a boardwalk, pigeons, solitary walkers, a giant Ferris wheel looming in the distance. We passed the liter back and forth between us.

When we stopped, he threw the bottle as far as he could into the sea. It bobbed for a few minutes before getting swallowed by a wave. We sat down cross-legged beside one another. He had told me the truth. He had led me to a place where it was very quiet. He lit a hand-rolled cigarette, which he passed to me as well.

I had maybe three or four drags before the light changed a little with a passing cloud. There was a solitary dog limping on the abandoned stretch of beach, and I tried to call her over to us. She looked very skinny, and I was remembering I had some potato chips in my backpack.

Dumb animal, he said.

Aw, she's just hungry, I said, digging in my bag for the potato chips.

Uh-huh, he said, but very slowly, and not taking his eyes off mine.

He leaned into me so fast and quick I fell onto my back in the sand.

Still, I made an effort to laugh through my nose, but I remember he didn't smile.

He kissed me on the mouth, and I kissed him back.

I wanted him in part because I liked the way he tasted and in part because I realized how alone we were, how there was no one else passing, how he was much stronger than me. I noticed the few white strands in his hair and in his beard.

I tried to keep the dog in my line of sight just over his shoulder—and for a while I saw her glancing back at me, each of us locked in a gaze that said to the other, I see you, I acknowledge your existence, living thing*—but after a while I lost track of her.*

At a certain moment, he stopped kissing me and he grinned at me with another look I could not name. I was busy trying to remember to enjoy the feeling of him, to convince myself that this was a decision I was making, that I had already made. I didn't try to stop him.

When he stood up and pulled on his shorts, he started up the beach without turning around. Words surfaced from my gut but stuck in my throat. I stayed behind and stared out into the waves. But not for long, because I realized I didn't know how to get back to the train. I stood quickly, and I trailed maybe a hundred meters behind him, kept the bobbing of his shoulders visible. He looked so free, the way he walked. I hated him and I desired him and I envied him all at once.

Sometimes when I watched you walk away from me, I thought of the way that stranger walked away from me. But I never told you this.

You were already starting to divide up within me then, but I didn't know it.

I felt sick to my stomach, and I couldn't get out of bed for days at a time. I slept like a corpse when I slept at all. But all that was foreign to me in the way that it made me feel less alone. If I threw up every fruit that I had eaten my entire life and digested without a problem, it was evidence of my being accompanied by you, you who had attached yourself to my body like a parasite, who did not have the same likes and dislikes as I did, you who did not blindly accept my preferences for breakfast without making your presence known. I felt something else, a little sinister and strange. I didn't know my own body. I considered that maybe I had turned into a witch, and I can't explain why I felt more myself than I ever had in my life.

If it weren't for that feeling, I'm not sure I would have kept you with me.

It was because of you that I missed the student demonstrations all that fall.

I was curled up in a ball on the bathroom floor of my mother's home. Otherwise, I would have been there when the National Guard showed up and started shooting rubber bullets into the crowd, and when all the most vocal members of the Department of Arts and Letters were rounded up in the backs of trucks and placed in detention. I am sure if you were not with me, I would have been with them.

In this way you encumbered me. You kept me home and heavy, unable to run.

But it was a time when running couldn't save anyone. I could hear at night the groans of the people who had tried to run, from within their cells, hidden within the capital, and in this way I understood what running had gotten them.

There is a history, in more places than I can count, of the children of resisters being reassigned to new mothers. I told myself, if I had been able to run, you would have been taken away from me. It was the kind of situation that the prophecies of the Book of Revelation got wrong, backward.

There are so many ways you saved me from suffering. There are other ways that I suffered more than I would have ever imagined possible because of you.

Like now for example.

It's a constant tally of pluses and minuses. But what life is not organized like this?

I hear a thud in the kitchen, and I walk away from the recording, as Rita continues to speak behind me.

Diane? I say.

A muffled reply moves me swiftly to the place where it came from.

I find her in a heap in front of the stove.

I slipped, she says.

How?

Balancing on a chair to reach the sugar bowl, she smiles. I'm okay.

But she doesn't look okay. I crouch by her side, and it takes all my strength to hoist her up and place her in a chair at the kitchen table.

Damn hip, she says.

I have made a cold compress, the way that Diane has instructed me to, with a plastic bag filled with frozen vegetables and a rubber band and a kitchen towel. I pass it to Diane, and she hitches up her skirt to fit the makeshift ice pack in place.

She is rubbing her hip, seated across from me under the brash light of the kitchen, and I notice that her face is wet.

Are you in a lot of pain? I ask.

Diane gazes straight ahead, makes no attempt to wipe the tears from her face. She nods, looks far away, like the fall has transported her to some fresh new place of hurt.

What is it? I ask.

I feel like I'm in a hole in the ground, she says, rubbing the ice pack into place again. A grave, she clarifies.

I sit still, to listen, but Diane doesn't elaborate.

I understand, from reading the mothers' stories, that grief is long work. It's a feeling that can come for you when you're reaching for the sugar bowl or walking to the bus stop. You can think you're outside of it, but you slip back in, like an ankle dipping fast into a divot in the grass, a quick bruise.

Diane says, I know that I may die before they return a piece of him to me.

She speaks to no one, to the space between us.

I say nothing. There is nothing to say. We keep sitting there under the harsh light of the kitchen.

By the time I return to the bedroom, I find my phone making a record of the dead air of the room.

III

III

FIELD NOTES

May 1

They start moving to the capital.

Not all at once. But slowly, one by one, they pick up and leave their towns and villages behind. They come when their new homes become too dangerous to stay. Or when the monthly math of making a living there no longer adds up. Or when they decide they have a better chance of some authority who cares taking note of the increased visibility of their demonstrations as their numbers grow.

Miriam filled a small handbag with a change of clothes and three pairs of underwear, also a locket that belonged to her mother. She imagines there is some physical relic of her mother inside the clasp—a lock of hair, a fingernail—but she's never opened it because she's anxious over losing what's inside, or because she avoids learning it's always been empty.

Eli boarded the bus with her backpack full of pastries, but this time, she didn't hop off before it pulled out of the station. Instead, she took a seat toward the back. When she got hungry, she ate the contents of her backpack, lightening her load little by little, the closer the bus inched toward the capital.

Juliet delayed for months. She'd hoped to travel with her mother to the capital, but her mother refused to displace herself again. Juliet didn't want to leave her mother behind. There were many arguments, threats, promises. But in the end, it's everyone for herself. Juliet made her decision, and her mother made hers. She came alone, and now she's as motherless as the rest of them.

Lira came because of her daughter. The threats had gotten worse, the phone calls more obscene. Lira's daughter Renata had started to grow her hair long and thick, and to brush it at night on the balcony, humming to herself under her breath. Everyone who heard her humming, anyone who caught sight of the devastating length of her hair understood. The callers knew about her hair, her humming. Lira arrived at Renata's school in a taxi with a small sack of her things prepared, and when her daughter broke away from her friends and looked at her mother bewildered, Lira said calmly, as if coaxing a wild animal into captivity, Don't worry, it's going to be okay. Just get in the car.

Lexus met a man who brought her here. He was a client at first, but they became close. It's no secret that he's the one who paid for her to come. He forgot about her later, but he also forgot her debt to him. Good luck and bad luck often come all at once like that, so it's hard to work out the true nature of someone's fortune.

Sofia said, I wasn't sure if I had it in me to pick up and move again. I swore I wouldn't, but it's not much more than a defense mechanism. It turns out that staying alive is an instinct, a reflex.

I never went home. At first it seemed that it would be in my best interest to return to my country and put greater distance between me and the events associated with the town where I collected testimonies—a town whose name has become synonymous in the national media with mass disappearances—but now so many of my informants have made their way to the capital that it hardly matters.

May 15

They live in the mountains, same as always. Their calf muscles are accustomed to the steady inclines. On clear days, they look down not on the river cutting through the land but onto the glimmering monuments that are the living towers.

They gaze down onto geometric order, understanding that the lucky ones will find work in these residences: cleaning the floors, cooking the rice, ironing the shirts of the people who live inside them but who are gone for many hours, who leave the towers empty, in need of working bodies to occupy them during the day.

The mothers remove their shoes before they step on the slick linoleum floors of the living towers. In their backpacks, they bring along a second pair of shoes, pristine, never worn outside. The soles of these shoes remain immaculate; they are made for gliding along the flooring of living towers while pushing a stick mop, without leaving a trace of dirt behind them. The mothers have never seen their feet look so delicate and soft; each day, in these shoes, they perform miracles, transformations. They erase the domestic disarray with the products provided and with their own hands. Like Cinderella and her fairy godmother at once.

June 3

It was Eli who told me that Queenie had come, that she had come
a long time ago. She had wandered off on her own for a while,
but several months later Queenie was spotted by one of the other
mothers in the settlements in the outskirts of the capital. She lives
in a peripheral neighborhood like the rest of them. She wasn't
talking much to anyone.

I found her where Eli said I could. I asked her if she was looking for work. She didn't want work, she said. But Eli and the others told me that she was desperate, that no one else would hire
her because of her limp.

When I found her, I asked her to come work for me.

Queenie is very proud, but she is not so proud that she'll let
herself starve to death.

That's how it came to be that we started spending every day
together in my living tower, writing these notes.

June 29

I watch Queenie. Technically I've hired her to be the caretaker of my apartment, to cook and clean for me while I'm at work. Thanks to the generous research stipend from the university, I've found that I can afford to pay Queenie for four full days of work, but because she is very efficient and because I'm not too fastidious we've found that she can take care of the bulk of the housework in a day and a half. This leaves Queenie two and a half days to sit on the balcony with coffee and cross-stich, or listen to the radio, or stare out into the mountains and on windy days observe the smoke from her cigarette drift in the direction of where her home once was.

At first, I didn't mention Zara.

July 11

Mostly, I barricade myself inside my office and leave her the run
of the apartment. I hear Queenie out there on the other side of the
door. Sometimes the sound of her rustling in the hallway is accompanied by the harsh smell of bleach. Other times, from the smell
of cigarettes wafting under the door, I imagine that she is smoking
inside the apartment. I mentioned to her that this is a nonsmoking
rental unit, but I don't insist on this rule when she breaks it.

On the days when she isn't cleaning, Queenie makes a lot of
juices. The whirr of the blender is often audible from my office.
Sometimes the juices she prepares turn out such unexpected colors, I want to ask what strange mix of fruits they are before taking
a sip from the extra glass that she left in the fridge for me. But
mostly I don't ask. I try to stay out of her way.

Once, when I emerged and took a big gulp from a bright
green juice, the shouts of children could be heard from the pool
in the courtyard.

I closed the fridge. Queenie opened the cupboard. We didn't
touch or speak, but I could feel her presence close by.

I heard a boy shout, Cannonball!

My eyes followed down to the splash that drove the other children to the perimeter of the pool. How old were they? I wondered. Fourteen? Thirteen?

She watched me watch them, taking in something, but I couldn't be sure what.

Thank you. I tipped my glass in her direction, as if toasting her. Delicious.

Queenie nodded, but she did not smile.

August 2

Eventually I learn to stop listening to my system of internal filtering. It would be painful for Queenie to speak, yes, but wasn't it also important for her to confront what had happened? In retrospect, I don't know why I felt an impulse to help her manage her grief, or where that arrogance came from.

It was a cool afternoon when I walked onto the balcony while she was sitting in a lawn chair out there and placed my hand on her shoulder.

I felt her stiffen immediately beneath my touch.

Do you mind if I sit? I asked her.

It's your house, Queenie said.

Are you comfortable here? I asked her.

Queenie looked me in the eye for the first time since I'd sat beside her, as if she were trying to see through me to something on the other side.

Comfortable, she repeated, like she was trying out the word for size.

I mean, I said, is there anything that you would like to have here, that would make you feel more at peace?

Queenie leaned back in her lawn chair. She stared off for a long time and I thought that she was mentally elsewhere, that she had left the conversation. I started to think about the responsibilities that would be necessary once I got back to my country, little tasks and hassles, when I heard her say, quietly under her breath, Yes.

Yes? I confirmed.

She said, I would like it if you would stop talking.

I went to the market the next day. I only knew that I wanted to come home with some kind of animal. There were rabbits, puppies, fish, turtles, lizards, and kittens for sale. I could have walked out with any of them.

The woman who worked in the stand seemed genuinely perplexed by my indecision. I can't make up your mind for you, she said. They're totally different species.

I paced the aisles and thought about lifespans. I wasn't sure how long each of the animals was expected to live.

Which one of these animals will take the longest to die? I asked.

Excuse me? the pet lady said.

I want an animal that's going to outlive me, I said.

Oh, then you better go with one of the birds, she said. They could survive the apocalypse.

August 16

The next time Queenie arrived at the apartment, the parrot's cage had been installed in the corner of the balcony. She finished her cleaning and sat in her usual spot. She started to settle into her chair and then shifted at the sound of a bristle of feathers. I watched her from behind the sofa on the other side of the open door.

What's this? she said.

Oh, this is Marylin.

Queenie scoffed, That bird is miserable.

I thought she looked like a good companion, I said, but I didn't say for whom.

I guess I figured it would be good for Queenie to have someone to talk to since she wasn't going to talk to me, but she doesn't speak much. She only sits out there as she always had before. It seems to have changed nothing.

Then one day she said, Actually, I thought of something.

Anything, I said.

I want to hear the tapes.

I didn't have to ask her which ones. The next day when she arrived, I'd set the tapes and the headset on the table on the balcony. She lifted the headset to her ears. There were maybe three hours of tapes that I thought would be of interest to her. But she stayed out there with the headphones on all day.

I spent the day writing in my office. I was making great progress and wrote with ease that hadn't been available to me in months. I felt absolutely in control of the shape the material assumed on the page. It wasn't until much later, once the sun had started to set, that I finally rose from my desk to turn on the lights and pour a glass of water. I walked from the office to the kitchen when I realized that she was no longer on the balcony.

Queenie? I called out onto the landing, into the living room. Queenie? I said, hushed now on the balcony, as if talking to the night. The tapes were gone, and so was the recording device. The parrot looked at me like I was a sucker. The lights of the surrounding mountains burned in the distance.

This is where the book ends. It was unfinished at the time of Rita Zapo's death.

—A.

A.

The next morning, my mother calls. My grandmother Marie, who said Hail Marys for each of her college credit hours and kept a rosary next to her remote control, died during the night.

I book the next flight home to the strip malls and cornfields. Technically, I am scheduled to stay for another month, but—as everyone knows—translating can be done from anywhere. It would be a gross overestimation of my project's importance to forfeit attending my own grandmother's funeral. Since I know it will be cost prohibitive to return before my visa expires, I say a few goodbyes.

In the last twenty-four hours prior to my departure, I go back to the Public Library of the People. I thank Edgar, and he grasps my hand in his usual courteous manner and shakes it to wish me well. I pay my roommates for the extra month, and they seem relieved.

By the time I arrive at the offices of Mothers United, they have already left for a demonstration outside the All Souls Cathedral, situated in the public square directly across from the capitol building.

*   *   *

In the square in front of All Souls, the banners that the mothers have been cross-stitching are gloriously unfurled. The banners' multicolor complexity is in sharp contrast to the mothers' white attire. They stand in rows and sing songs at high volume about the intrinsic worth of a mother's love and the cowardly attitude of actors of the state. Some people hurry past, covering their ears as if their songs were discordant explosions. Others pause in their busy lives to recognize the mothers with solemn but firm applause. The clapping sounds syncopated and lonely, coming from individuals at different times, spaced out around the enormity of the square.

The mothers are early enough in the setup of their demonstration that they catch a few stragglers into the capitol building. A senator with salt-and-pepper hair exits a long black sedan and attempts to cross the square undetected. His pressed shirt and patent-leather shoes immediately identify him as someone who works inside the capitol, but he attempts to take cover behind a manila folder raised in his right hand as he inches across the sea of people. He does not go unnoticed.

Jasmin is holding the megaphone, leading a song. When she sees the senator with salt-and-pepper hair cross the square, she changes the lyrics of the hymn to publicly ridicule him.

Coward, coward! the mothers chant in chorus between each of Jasmin's proclamations.

Diane is standing in the shade when I find her between songs. She grasps my hand.

I wanted to thank you, I say.

Of course, honey.

And to let you know I'm going home tomorrow.

She nods, unfazed.

I didn't expect to leave so soon, I say. My grandmother is dead.

Sweetie, Diane says, you don't have to explain anything to me.

She opens her arms to me, offers an embrace.

I hug her politely, but then more fiercely, and as I breathe in the fabric of her white summer sweater, I am sobbing into her chest. I am crying for my grandmother and for Diane's son, and for Rita and for Rita's son. I am crying for the loss of the possibility of my body ever being the home to another.

I don't have the right, I say between sobs. My grandmother was eighty-five.

Diane says, No such thing as a right.

She plants a kiss on my hairline, gently, like a mother.

But tears don't help, Diane says, straightening her posture.

As I take a step back, I hear her voice join the chorus of the other mothers assailing two new senators crossing the square on their way toward the capitol building.

Because the rest of the family is busy with funeral preparations, it is my other grandmother, Leonora, who picks me up from the airport. At ninety-three, she is an expert driver. She takes the back roads to avoid the expressway, but more out of a courtesy to those of us who worry about her on the road than out of any lack of ability to keep up with traffic.

Welcome home, she says, from the driver's seat, as I load my suitcase into her trunk.

She wears oversize, cheap plastic sunglasses, and her short gray curls closest to the window blow in the wind. She is just shy of double the age of most of the mothers, I think.

Did you have a nice time? she asks.

I stiffen for a moment before I nod.

On the day of the funeral, all the photographs of my grand-mother Marie flood the room. When she is my age, she is inside of a torpedo of children, their diapered butts, their dangling legs, their open books of math homework. She looks serene, but fierce, at once. Her eyes have the luminous gaze of someone who hasn't gotten a good night's sleep in a decade.

The last time I saw her, I pushed her wheelchair through the chaos of a large family gathering. I talked to her for a few minutes, explaining irrelevant details about my life in the city, just to fill the silence.

Are you still watching baseball on television? I asked her.

She smiled.

You don't miss a game of the World Series, I bet.

She smiled.

Do you think we have a chance this year? I asked.

My grandmother shrugged her shoulders and made her eyes smile again. In her eyes there was still a kind of resolve, grace.

Her look said, I know you don't know anything about base-ball.

* * *

At the funeral, everyone looks like they haven't slept in decades but don't carry it as well: We all have puffy bags under our eyes, smeared eye makeup.

Everyone at the microphone runs through the litany: the mother of ten, the grandmother of twenty-nine, the great-grandmother of a growing number more.

After the cemetery, we overrun my grandmother's small kitchen with our fifty-plus adult bodies. It's the same place where she raised ten, then watched baseball games alone. So now the kitchen feels like a brimming glass of something threatening to spill over the sides.

My aunts tell stories: The time she drove the family station wagon to the grocery store and back with a mug of coffee on the roof and didn't spill a drop. The time she pulled the same car up alongside her twelve-year-old son walking home from school with a cigarette dangling from his mouth and asked him if he wanted a ride. The time she awoke in the night to angels speaking of recipes to her and tried to prepare the dishes the next day.

Later, they ask me: How long are you in town for? Where do you live again? Remind me how you make a living?

I try to answer their questions, even if I don't always know the words to fill out the gaps in my story. I have been away from home for so long that it's hard not to feel like an interloper, eavesdropping on my own family's mythology.

The next day, my mother, my other grandmother—Leonora—
and I go shopping.

You're here for so few days, my mother says, We should take
advantage, I mean, while we're all together.

It's the three of us, then: my grandmother, who picked onions
for loose change the summer before the war; my mother, who went
to college and navigated her way through motherhood, homeown-
ership, a stable middle-class life; and me.

The ritual begins, as it always does, with the three of us in my
mother's gray Volvo station wagon: My mother drives, I am in the
passenger seat beside her, and my grandmother, nestled in the
back seat behind us, hums along with the radio.

Where should we start? my mother asks, rhetorically.

The glamorous department stores of my childhood, places like
Marshall Field's, are long extinct, or no longer are what they once
were, and we rarely frequent them. We always start at the same
places, the places we can find discounts: Marshalls, T.J. Maxx,
Nordstrom Rack. The stores where you might find underwear,
luggage, and Himalayan sea salt cozied up against each other in a
single aisle. The stores that demand patience to rummage hanger
by hanger through the racks, holding up an occasional item to

assess its worth. The stores that offer a large and complicated history on every price tag: what the full retail price was once, how much has been taken off over a series of markdowns. When we find a price significantly below retail value on an article of clothing that fits one of us, we are overcome with exhilaration. We will find a use for the article of clothing: We will wait for the seasons to change, we will lose weight, we can dress up more, we will get the right underwear to make it work, we will start standing up straight.

After scouring the racks, riffling through items unworthy of our attention, we find a pile of contenders to ferry into the fitting rooms, each of us with a neat stack of clothes slung over our forearms, waiting for the attendant who will solemnly count them out under her breath and offer us a corresponding laminated number to hang outside the fitting room door.

We speak through the walls that divide us, as we try on the first few items.

How do the pants fit? I hear my mother ask my grandmother.

A little snug, not sure.

Make sure you remember to try to sit down in them in there.

I'll show you in a minute, says my grandmother.

When we come out to model items for one another, we linger in the common area, comment on necklines, waistlines, lengths, cuts. Eventually we abandon the partitions between us and float freely between one another's fitting rooms.

As we examine the tags announcing the provenance of each item, we call to mind places that are hot and wet, dry and mountainous; we call to mind rows of women sewing seams shut. Still, it makes us feel better to have a new dress to slip on or a pair of jeans that fits. It makes us feel less alone, less powerless in the face of disappointments in our bodies or the things we cannot control in our lives.

When I pass a short black dress over my head, it clings to my body. It feels divine.

As I step out of the dressing room, I hear my mother tsk.

Too short for work, she says, though I don't have a job anymore.

I wander farther into the hallway between the shuttered doors of the dressing rooms, until I reach the triptych of mirrors at the end, under the glow of the fluorescent lights. In my socks, I prep for a turn. I turn to my left, then to my right. I watch my hips shift in the mirror as I step forward, then back.

I walk from the bathrooms at the back of the store, and when I return to the line, I see that Leonora is excitedly talking to a woman beside her who looks to be in her eighties.

I just turned ninety-three, she says proudly to the woman.

I look to my mother, and she just shifts her eyes toward the ceiling. This look says, No, of course they don't know each other.

Leonora forges a kinship with a new woman in every store. She always finds someone willing. She lives alone. Walking malls and strip malls is her routine, regardless of what she buys. These are the best places to run into other women of her generation.

As I listen in on the conversation, I watch Leonora hold a sweater up to the woman's chest as if checking the size for her.

Sure, you could dress this up or down, Leonora says. Depends on the shoes and the jewelry. It's versatile, you know.

The woman replies, also gesturing emphatically toward the sweater.

That's when I notice that the woman and my grandmother are not speaking the same language.

Leonora long ago has lost the language of her parents, but she says she still can find her way inside it when she hears it spoken by someone else. Along with this seems to come the ability to understand any foreign language of which she has no working knowledge. If she doesn't share a language with someone, it only makes her gestures bigger, her embraces more fierce. By the time I pay for my items and push my basket to nestle back into a row of carts, Leonora has her arms wrapped around the other woman, and the woman clings to Leonora, their hands clutching one another like sisters.

That night, while I'm packing my suitcase, my mother knocks on my door. When I open it, she gestures to my shopping bag in the corner.

What did you end up with? she asks.

The black dress, a blouse, a pair of jeans, I say.

I don't think I saw the jeans on, she says.

I shrug. Do you want me to try them?

Only if you want a second opinion, honey, she says.

Okay, I say. Sure.

I slither out of my sweatpants and stand in my underwear rummaging in the bag for the jeans. Forty percent off, I say, reading from the tag, and another fifteen at the register.

Oh, that is really good, my mother nods.

I slip one leg into them, then another, and button the fly and lean forward into the mirror above the dresser in my childhood bedroom. Behind me, I see her reflection. Her lips are pursed like she's studying the fit. Her eyes look tired, but they flicker with activation by the task at hand.

They're great, she says, smiles.

Yeah, I say. I thought so.

You could stay, she says. You don't even really have a job there anymore. I mean, you don't have to go back.

I know, I say. But I do.

I can't explain why. I feel guilty about being more at home hundreds of miles away from where I was raised, in a place where I am completely anonymous, where there is no one to give an honest critical assessment of anything I wear or say or do. But because I don't know how to voice this feeling, I let it stay unspoken between us as I continue to fold and fit my things into my suitcase.

The following night, while unpacking into the narrow closet of a room I've rented in the city, I find a Post-it note cozied between my books (*Be safe! XOXO, your mom*), and for a week straight I feel momentarily homesick each time I glance at it stuck to the wall above my desk, until I finally remove it from the wall and tuck it quietly between two pages of Rita Zapo's book. For safe-keeping, I tell myself.

Returning to the city is harder than I anticipated. Having relinquished the lease to my studio apartment prior to my departure, my only option is to rent a room with strangers far from the city center. I find a job as a copy editor, working remotely. I rent a room that becomes my sleeping, eating, and work space. The room costs a little over half of what I make copyediting, but that is what starting over looks like. I cannot afford health insurance, and I feel myself fleetingly relieved that the regular surveillance of my reproductive organs is in my past.

My roommates and I do not interact much, though occasionally we find ourselves preparing dinner at the same time in the kitchen. We are courteous and respectful to a fault. I am the only one who is from this country, but everyone has internalized the individualism of daily life here quickly, maybe even better than I have.

In the fridge we each have a dedicated shelf for our produce and dairy products. My shelf is the middle one. I shop multiple times a week to fill my designated space. We each have our own salt, our own olive oil, our own quart of milk.

It makes my teeth hurt to buy small portions of everything and then replace them. It makes my teeth hurt to write my initials on oversize items that are placed in the swinging door of the fridge.

The people in this country write their initials on their quarts of milk, I think sadly, remembering my students, wondering if they are still living here, writing their initials on their quarts of milk in other apartments, or whether they went back to their birth cities, whether their observations served them to carve out a place for themselves here or only to underscore the unsustainability and the foreignness of this place.

I think of my students as I watch my roommates wash the dishes, hear them talking in their own languages behind their closed bedroom doors, coming out to make their dinners-for-one, turning off the water between rinsing each utensil and glass.

When I go to the apartment building to visit R., the doorman smiles.

Going to 4G? he asks.

Yes, I say.

Go on up, he says.

I have been gone for five months, and I am still part of the repertoire of nonresidents who have unquestioned access to the building. I wonder how long I would have to be away for the doorman to cease to recognize me, for my face to blend with the face of any woman with a messy ponytail on top of her head, approaching the building with her umbrella in her hand.

His waving me up feels like a kind of belonging, a signal that the city has not forgotten me.

R. and his mother are sitting in the middle of a small carpet in the living room when I open the door.

Hello? I say, approaching slowly.

R.'s mother knew that I was stopping by, but for R. my presence is unexpected. Unlike the doorman, he looks up and seems to be sorting through files in the back office of his brain, trying to match me up with a memory of me.

He stands up, and I crouch down ready to receive one of his long hugs, but he walks past me, goes to his room, and shuts the door firmly.

Hey! his mom says through the closed door. That wasn't very nice.

It's okay, I say to R.'s mom. She brings me a glass of water. I sit down on the sofa across from her, and we start to talk about R.'s new caretaker, the classes she's teaching, the prices of rents in the city.

Several minutes later, R. comes out of his room with a book in his hand. It is one of our favorites, about the townspeople who were terrified of the lion and the boy who saves him. R. points to the book and he points to me.

Is that what you were looking for in your room? R.'s mom asks him.

I think about the lion, how much safer he feels away from the fears of the townspeople. I press my mouth to the crown of R.'s head as he settles himself beside me on the couch with the book on his lap.

220

At first, I do not go dancing. I have in my muscle memory the torque it takes to spin on linoleum and hardwood and concrete, the relative tension and promise of a strong or a weak lead in my biceps, the calculations of the length of steps to fit in different venues based on the size of the floor, the quantity of bodies. I remember the rhythm of the final songs, when the night is almost over, when most of the dancers have gone home. I savor all this in the tendons of my legs. But, still, I do not dance anywhere but in my bedroom, alone at night, just before I go to sleep.

Skinny, I sometimes think to myself. Skinny, skinny, skinny.

But I repeat it over and over again, until it is meaningless, a sound with no head or tail. Like odd tissues, chromosomes that blossom but fail to grow into something more.

Lying in bed that night, I scroll through my phone to distract myself from the sounds of *skinny, skinny, skinny* that collide through my brain. I find a smattering of photos that I took: A smear of lights out the window of the businessman's hotel. A duller smear out the window of my apartment. My face in a filthy bathroom mirror. The mothers' tapestry that says REPENT, COWARDS! hanging in the tree outside a gaggle of municipal buildings.

I open the voice memos and see the file named RITA. I hit PLAY and hear Rita's voice begin to speak. The thud in the kitchen. My voice calling for Diane, getting further away. Then Rita's voice keeps talking as my footsteps patter toward the kitchen.

It's been months. I don't even know why I'm writing to you anymore. The last time we spoke, you were angry. I don't remember why.

Okay, I do remember why.

You were angry with me.

I lied to you.

About your father and other things.

But that's why I'm trying to come clean in writing you, hoping these letters reach you.

I lied to protect you. This is the root source of all lies. You're old enough now to know that.

Do you remember how happy we were when we lived those first years of our lives together in your grandmother's home? At first, there was nothing to do but wait for things to get better. I fed you, watched you, and wrote letters. I listened to the radio. I waited for news, for you to grow, for the situation to shift. I read you books and played with you on the balcony of my mother's apartment.

In the evenings while you slept, I started writing again.

I was lucky I had access to the trappings of a middle-class life. I was living off money that wasn't mine.

By the time you were old enough to go to school, we started winning prizes. We started getting invitations to travel to festivals here and there, festivals where people talked about the violence at home in terms that were both flippant and hyperbolic at once.

I say we, in spite of the fact that I was the one who won the prizes and traveled to the foreign cities. You, I mostly left at home with my mother. You had school. I thought it was better for you to be in one stable place, on firm ground. I thought I'd have more time to spend with you once I was better established. I imagine now what it was to be the one who was always left at home waiting.

I used to yell at you for being wasteful, for acting like we owned the electric company and could use as much energy as we liked, but the truth is this: I miss the way you used to open the door of the fridge and stare, like the cold air was going to give you some kind of code you could use in the kid world you lived in.

When you were thirteen years old, you became someone else, someone new. You had a side that was sharper and not fully comprehensible to me. I blamed myself for leaving you alone so much in my mother's apartment.

You had a skateboard, and you spent afternoons when you should have been in school clinging to railings with your four wheels and skidding down staircases outside the mall.

We fought, I know you will remember how bitterly we fought, when I found out you were ditching school to roll around on four wheels. But it wasn't the ditching school I objected to.

The mall had been a prison, a site of interrogation and torture. When I rocked you to sleep as a child, we could hear the moaning voices of the detained. Everyone knew where they were coming from, from the prison that became a mall—they didn't even change the facade, to try to mask the barbarity in some way—and you, skating down railings and jumping the staircases, like it was nothing.

Later, I didn't know how to care for you. I didn't understand the things I should have. I wanted you to be different than you were. I didn't want you to ask so many questions, I didn't want you to remind me of things I wanted to forget.

I told you your father was not from the capital. I told you he was someone I met on a trip to his country when I was young. I didn't explain that I didn't know him really, aside from his name, his city, and the few details I could still conjure up. I didn't want you to think you had come into the world through an act of violence. Though he wasn't violent.

The morning I realized you were gone, I went to the office of the local police precinct to file a missing person report.

Take a number, they said. Take a seat.

I waited in their office for a long time, looking around at the others. There was a man who kept methodically taking his wallet out, thumbing through what was there, and replacing it in his back pocket. A wiry young woman smoked a cigarette every twenty minutes. On the television in the corner, a program on the predatory habits of swamp animals played without sound. According to the program's captions for the hearing impaired, swamp species were resilient in ways other members of the animal kingdom couldn't begin to comprehend.

When is the last time you saw the missing person? the police asked me when I finally made it into their office.

This morning, I said. He left for school.

Full name?

I gave the officer your name, and he repeated it slowly, as if it was a foreign word.

Age?

Nineteen.

Any possible motive for him to run away?

I shifted in my seat. I shook my head.

What's your relationship to the boy's father? the official asked, not looking up from the form.

Nonexistent, I said.

The official glanced over the form at me.

It would be a good idea to contact the father if you can.

That's impossible, I said.

You went to the city to look for your father. I know that much. You were nearly the age that I was when I boarded the plane that led me to you.

I stop the tape. I rewind it. I listen again.

The following week, another boy is killed in another nearby town. He has black skin, loose clothes, and a toy gripped fiercely in his hand, which he refuses to drop when requested to do so by the police. Again, everyone takes to the streets. I make a sign with a piece of poster board and a marker. I walk alongside the demonstrators. I sing the chorus of each call and response chant. There are thousands of us out on the street in the city. Some people walk, some people shout encouragement from their fire escapes, some people hand out bottles of water.

Some people's poster boards contain laminated photos of murdered men and boys.

REPENT, COWARDS! I think to myself, I cross-stich in my mind.

When the demonstration breaks up, I turn a corner down a residential street. It is then that I see a girl with a shock of black curls. She rides by on a boy's bike. She passes by so quickly at first.

She passes again and again, like she's trying to learn to ride.

I shake my head. I think, Zara is dead.

But she looks so real to me and so much like Zara does in my mind, with her scraped-up, skinny knees and chapped lips, with her fat tires and her eyes squinting into the sunshine.

* * *

The girl does a quick turn and her tire catches in a crack in the sidewalk. She falls hard, and I run over to where she's hit the ground. By the time I reach her, the girl has already hoisted herself up to a sitting position. Her knee is bleeding, but she doesn't cry. Are you okay? I ask. I rustle through my purse in pursuit of a Band-Aid.

The girl looks down at her knee, as she opens her mouth to speak.

I am not allowed to talk to strangers, she says, almost mechanically, as if repeating something by rote.

Here, I say, just take this. I outstretch my arm, placing the small Band-Aid in her field of vision, just in front of her skinned knee.

I am also not allowed to accept anything from strangers, the girl says.

Okay, I say. Is there someone I can call from home who could come and help you?

She meets my eyes like she thinks I might be dangerous or stupid.

I'm not giving you my home phone number, the girl says.

Then she picks up her bike and stumbles down the street toward home.

The following night, I take a taxi to the basement bar of Ciel. My muscles are vibrating under my skin as soon as I am within three feet of the door.

The bouncer smiles at me, Long time. Where have you been, beautiful?

I pay the woman sitting between the front bar and the back bar five dollars to pass through the heavy velvet curtain behind her. I hold out my wrist to her and savor the feeling of the stamp biting down on my skin. It is eleven o'clock on a Thursday night, and there are hundreds of people sweating in time with the music. I try to maintain composure, looking objectively at what this is: people stepping in patterns they've learned, the drums dictating their tempo. But within minutes, the corners of my mouth break through, and my teeth are visible, and I can't hold back the sense of an unfiltered dose of some powerful chemical.

I sit and watch for the length of the rest of the song that plays when I walk in. The couple in front of me create a game of it, mimicking each other's steps, each time he releases her. She stays close, follows him with her eyes even as she spins away from him.

The next song, I am approached by a man I don't know. He

has large hands and very white teeth. He asks me my name, and I ask him his.

When I feel his pull forward into the space of the song, I stutter, but only for a moment. It has been a long time since I have been inside Ciel, and I feel overstimulated and distracted. I am watching every person around me move, and I am singing the words of the song, and I am feeling the leads of the man with large hands as he invites me into turns.

After the song ends, I am bent over the bar drinking a big gulp from my water bottle, when I feel a pull on my wrist that I recognize. I know it is N. before I hear him speak.

Skinny? he barely whispers.

I say nothing, but I turn slowly and take him in.

He looks smaller, like a room that used to be familiar often does when you walk into it after some time away. He takes my hand into his and leads me toward a clearing in the floor.

My mind protests, but my muscles override.

His eyes stay on mine for several moments. He does not start to dance. Instead, he holds us both perfectly still in the middle of all the other swaying bodies.

Then he steps back and pulls my body into the void in front of him. I clasp my left hand around his shoulder, but only for a moment, and soon we're moving quickly. He's launched me away, and I spin and spin. Out of the corner of my eye, I see his mouth is moving, and then I can hear that he is singing the lyrics under his breath: off-key, as always, and it makes me feel sad for a minute that he probably doesn't know how terribly he sings.

The lyrics are about a man whose life is over: His brother is killed, his mother disowns him, his woman left him. He has no reason to go on living. But when he hears the music, he decides that he will live anyway, because of his terrible luck or in spite of it.

I sing the lyrics too, under my breath, as I always do.

Then, the song invites me inside of it; there is no need to think, because the beat is bigger than I am and reverberates in my tendons and muscles. I catch a turn. I feel his lead and I respond to it, in time, without compromising the next turn, which is his. And suddenly I can feel a measure of music stretch out into an indeterminate amount of time, large enough to stall the present so I can see it for the fleeting thing it is. But stalled like that in song, the present moment becomes distilled in my hips and in the ends of my fingers and in my feet, and I can feel enough to see clearly for a fraction of a second.

Then, just as suddenly, the song ends. N. drapes his long arm over my shoulder.

I missed you, skinny, he says. As if we could just fall back into a routine that quickly.

I take a step back, instinctively, away from him.

N. says, I told you I was sorry.

No, I say. You never did.

I can feel a prickling behind my eyes. I back up and turn around, and suddenly I have an impulse to flee. I have an impulse to not let N. see me cry. Gathering up my water bottle and my bag, I slip through the heavy velvet curtain and to the other side of the bar as fast as I can. As I make it to the street, I can feel him following me, but I don't turn around.

I start to walk. I feel angry and I feel lost. I want him to keep following me, and I want to break loose and run to another street, another city, another space-time continuum, where I never have to see him again.

I walk through the door of the closest diner, and I sit down in a booth. I see the waitress nod, and I manage a half smile and then stare into the laminated page of the menu until all the entrées become a blur. By the time N. reaches the booth, the tears have broken over the barrier of my eyelids and fall freely down my cheeks.

Do you need a minute? the waitress says, retreating.

No, N. says quietly. He passes the laminated menus back into her hand, saying, Two chamomile teas and a large order of french fries, please.

Before he opens his mouth again. Before I grow too angry. Before it's too late, I think.

I have something to show you, I say to N.

My phone is nestled into the pocket of my bag, and I hesitate for only a moment before fishing it out, opening my voice memos, and setting the phone on the table between us. I hit PLAY.

I hear the static, and then I hear Rita's voice start to speak.

Her question begins as if she were interviewing one of the other mothers, but it is when she starts to answer the question herself that N.'s eyes fill.

I press PAUSE and restart the tape.

He pulls out his own phone and hits RECORD.

Two chamomile teas and a large fry, says the waitress at some point, cautiously moving each item from her tray onto the table between us, between our phones flat on the table before us, disappearing fast.

We both keep our eyes on our twin phones in the center of the table. We have the same phone, as everyone in the city does. We watch the two phones—one speaking and one making a record. We watch the corner of the table, each other's crossed arms, elbows, freckles, fingernails, the buttons of our shirts, the hairs on our arms.

The tea is getting cold.

Neither of us moves.

I'm sorry. I know it isn't fair to compare you to the other boys. I know you left out of your own volition. I know it isn't the same to compare what happened to the other mothers to what happened to me.

But the small seed of pain growing in me with every day you're gone makes me care more about their boys. I know that it's selfish. I know that I wrote different kinds of poems before when I was more concerned with metaphor and meter than missing boys.

But isn't it the same for everyone? You don't know what loss is like until you lose your own. It's all abstract until you feel it inside your bones.

As I listen, I think about Lexus in the laundromat, crushing Milo's shirt into her face, finding new smells that linger with time. I think about Juliet sharing a bed with her mother, and all the other women who don't dare meet her eyes.

Sofia and Miriam and Eli.

I think about Queenie, her slow walk with a limp.

I close my eyes and I hear crickets. I see smears of stars. Of lights. The mothers of the mothers. The small dirt circles carved out by the tires of Zara's bike.

I hear a sniffle, quickly stifled. N. drags his shirtsleeve along his nose.

When I look across the table, his eyes look wet, red-rimmed.

I search for the eyes of the boy who asked his mother if the bird poem she was writing was really about him. I have never found this poem. But now, in my mind, I can imagine N., across the table from his mother, a blue crayon steady in his hand, poised to shift into the shape of the story she tells him.

When you were five years old, I took you to see a traveling circus that had made a stop in a dusty beach town a few days' drive from home.

I can still see how all the kids sat cross-legged on the grass around us, whining while they waited for the show to begin. Their parents offered us their smiles. You sat still with rapt attention toward the spotlight on the empty sand floor, waiting for someone to walk into it.

The circus was world class: jugglers, clowns, gymnasts, a ringmaster with a shiny gold cloak and a top hat who pulled gold coins from the ears of the children in the first rows. When he pulled a coin from your ear, I watched your eyes dilate and dart around looking for explanations. You rubbed the lobe as if trying to recreate the magic yourself.

But we agreed that the most amazing of all was an acrobat, a one-woman act. She took the stage with a long piece of fabric, like a silken rope, that she stretched from the peak of the tent to its dusty floor, and began to scale it. She had painted eyes, dark skin, and a tight stomach that was visible in her skimpy costume.

When she reached the tent's apex, she started to let herself fall, little by little, but always it turned out that, secretly, she had been tying knots into the fabric, knots that were undecipherable to the eyes of her audience.

We kept waiting for her body to smash against the dirt floor of the tent, but the knots she'd tied caught her each time she plummeted: by the ankle, by the hips, by both wrists bound together.

Her glistening muscles barely twitched under the spotlight while we cooed and cheered for her to start her climb again. Each time she survived her fall, our desire increased to see her fall faster, survive more unexpectedly and gracefully. Her body appeared suspended for several seconds, inches from the imagined crash replaying in each of our brains, whenever it caught a knot. It was hard not to imagine the thousand times she smacked into the ground rehearsing for this moment, because now, under the spotlight of the tent, she was suspended triumphant, so still her body gave away only the most involuntary signs of breathing.

Later, at home, you approached me with serious eyes. You said, Mom, I want to be her.

You want to be who, honey? I said.

The acrobat, Mom, you said.

When I think of how you watched her with so much respect and wonder, my heart feels like it is too big for my chest, like it cannot be accommodated by barriers of muscle and bone.

N. takes a sip of his tea, like he needs the medicine of it now, but his eyes stay trained on our phones.

In the recording, I hear the thud in the kitchen and my footsteps pattering away.

I remember how in that moment, I found Diane in a heap on the floor.

Damn hip, she had said, and everything that followed.

Rita speaks on.

I don't know if you remember how you saved my life when you were just a boy. It was your call that alerted the neighbor. Without it I would have stayed closed up in the shower. It took a long time to learn to live again.

That morning, I nearly died in the shower. I woke up and I looked in the mirror, half-dressed, and I turned on the water. I don't know why I was half-dressed before I decided to take a shower, but this is how it happened. I turned on the water and stuck in my hand to gauge the temperature. Then, I felt the sharp pain, the one that told me to grasp onto the tiles. Instead, I only felt the slipperiness of the tiles beneath my foot, and I knew it was only a matter of time, and it was only then that I could hear you making noise in the other room beneath the sound of the shower. You were in the kitchen playing on the floor. With the dogs? I remember thinking at first. No . . . With a pot and a pan and a wooden spoon. I could hear you pounding away on all the different registers and notes, singing a child's song without words in any language, as my body started to slip on the surface of the tiles, as I started to wobble backward, and I knew that you would hear the thump of my body, and you would pause in your song and you would come to the bathroom, and you would

*say, Mama? Mom? I heard your feet coming toward me, down
the hall and into the bathroom. I kept still near the drain when I
felt the hiccup and surge inside my chest. My heart outgrew me.
The light started to flicker out just before it got bigger, brighter. I
waited for you.*

When the only sound left on the recording is the dead air in the room, I hit STOP.

Did you know she wrote *Field Notes*? I ask him.

Of course, he says.

Did any of her letters ever make it to you?

No, he says.

We look at each other for a long time.

Why did you disappear? I ask.

He keeps staring at me, then switches to a point just over my shoulder. He half shrugs, half shakes his head.

Why did you? he says.

He says, Skinny.
I close my eyes.
I'm sorry, he says.

I tip my mug back into my throat. I swallow the chamomile in several quick gulps, like a remedy that needs to get down quick.

I stand and N. stands. He opens his arms, and I embrace him.

I take his book out of my bag, and I place it on the table.

He shakes his head but does not speak.

He whispers into my ear, and I whisper into his.

I whisper in his language, and he whispers in mine.

As I turn to go, I sense his eyes follow me out the door. But he will remain rooted to the spot where he will finish his chamomile tea and pay the bill for us both. I have faith in this as I break away from his arms, from the gaze of the waitress, from the harsh fluorescent light of the diner, and into the night.

Outside, the night air whips around my ears and my hips and my fingers, and I feel I could walk forever.

I walk past the glowing lights of Ciel, where the dancers will spin and shimmy for several hours more before the music stops. I walk past the glowing billboards, blinking neon outside the classroom where I used to give night classes, where my students would nod and scribble into their notebooks.

Bypassing the train, I keep walking.

The glittering skyscrapers, still ahead in the distance.

Approaching the dark expanse of the park, I imagine animals burrowed in holes or in hovels, blinking into the night air.

Taxis slowing, honking, slowing, honking.

A memory of Diane saying, Now I walk at any hour of the night with my bad hip and all. I am afraid of nothing. This is the price of fearlessness.

I cross a bridge.

I walk toward the neighborhood where I live now, where, when I arrive, I will pour a glass of milk from the carton with my initials scrawled onto the side, where my roommates all sleep behind closed doors in their different rooms and dream in their different languages, where I will splash cold water on my face and climb into my own bed and dream of a girl on a bike, making slow circles, steady on the pedals, her eyes trained on the road.

ACKNOWLEDGMENTS

Although this story unfolds in fictional settings, its inception took shape, in part, thanks to two Tinker Foundation Field Research Grants I received, to Uruguay (2014) and Colombia (2015), while I was a graduate student in Latin American Studies at Tulane University. It never would have been written without my exposure to books, films, archives, and generous individuals willing to speak with me in Montevideo, Medellín, and New Orleans.

The testimonies throughout the novel are inspired by, but do not replicate, stories I encountered in research, with one exception. The quotation that Tomas Petritus and Rita Zapo argue over the right to reprint without permission is my direct translation of a testimony that appears in the exhibit *Ausencias* at the Museo Casa de la Memoria, in Medellín. I chose to include a record of one authentic voice in this work of fiction to remember global victims of displacement and violence whose lived experiences are not dissimilar to those this novel describes. The original quote, in its entirety, reads, "Perdí mi finca. Perdí mi pie derecho. Arriba de la rodilla. Y perdí el hogar. —Fabián."

Thank you to the Biblioteca Pública Piloto de Medellín para América Latina and the Universidad de la República's Centro de Estudios Interdisciplinarios Uruguayos for helping facilitate my research. I am grateful to the Madres de la Candelaria for sharing their stories with me.

At Tulane, I would like to thank: Yuri Herrera, my mentor and first reader, for generous conversations and early guidance; as well as Fernando Rivera and Zachary Lazar for their suggestions and support; my first-draft readers and friends Jimena Codina and Alex Santana; my program director James D. Huck Jr.; and professors Antonio Gómez, Guadalupe García, and Idelber Avelar. To Ignacio Sarmiento for editing every paper I ever wrote and Aroldo Nery Mora for all the fiction-writing side conversations and reading recs, and to Vanessa Castañeda for being my New Orleans rock. To the editors at *Boston Review* for publishing an early excerpt as a part of its Global Dystopias project.

Years later: my agent, Chris Clemans, restored my faith with his brilliant intuition and copious notes. I am indebted to everyone on the team at Henry Holt, including Leela Gebo and my editors: first Caroline Zancan, who gave my novel a home and patiently helped me reimagine parts I couldn't quite see, and then Riva Hocherman, for whose conviction and sage final notes I am extraordinarily grateful. Thank you to Jane Haxby for such a detailed copyedit.

Michael Zapata has been this book's greatest champion for a decade; Libby Garland offered her always-wise counsel and a place to live for several months when I most needed it; Eric Lundgren, Teddy Wayne, and Eileen G'Sell gave invaluable feedback and advice as readers and friends. Thank you for many conversations and much kindness at different moments throughout these years: Brian Gilman, Jordana Mendelson, Alicia Josten Zapata, Rachel Blustain, Matías Bosch Carcuro, Leonardo Certuche, Mauricio Higuera, Sarai Fonseca, Christine Mladic, and Sarah Ferone.

Most of all, thank you to my family for their love, support, and solidarity: to my father, James, and my mother, Jeanine, for believing in this book when she was one of its only readers; to my brothers, David and Michael; to Amanda and Maddy; to Andrés and María Pilar; to Marta and Almudena; and to Edie. To my grandmother Eleanor and in memory of my grandmother Rosemary.

To Andrés and Ezio: When I started on the journey of this project long ago, I didn't dare imagine the gift of finishing it alongside you both.

ABOUT THE AUTHOR

Sarah Bruni is a graduate of the MFA program at Washington University in St. Louis and holds a master's in Latin American studies from Tulane University. She has taught English and writing classes in New York and St. Louis, and she has volunteered as a writer-in-schools in San Francisco and Montevideo, Uruguay. She is also the author of the novel *The Night Gwen Stacy Died*. Her fiction has appeared in *Boston Review*, and her translations have appeared in the *Buenos Aires Review*. She lives in Chicago with her family.